ROCK

BOTTOM

Latasha Boyd

ROCK BOTTOM

The overall writing of this novel is a work of fiction with some references to events that are based on a true story. In order to maintain their anonymity in some instances I have changed the names of individuals and places, I may have changed some identifying characteristics and details such as physical properties, occupations and places of residence.

Author: Latasha Boyd
ISBN-13: 978-0692799611
ISBN-10: 0692799613
LCCN: TBD

Editing/Typesetting: Young Dreams Publications – Ty Waller
www.youngdreamsbig.com

Cover Design: POSH ANNOUCEMENTS for Young Dreams Publications

Connect with Latasha Boyd

Latashaboyd44@yahoo.com

Facebook: www.facebook.com/latasha.boyd.56

Twitter: @rockbottom_lb

Acknowledgments

First, I have to thank God for allowing me the focus, stamina, persistence, and faith to finish this project. So many times I wanted to give up but he saw me through it. I also have to thank Debra Morris for sharing her painful story with me. I thank her for being candid and patient in allowing me the time and freedom to complete this project. I also thank Eric Sears for allowing me to include him in this story.

I thank my loving husband Robert for his unrelenting love and support and for stepping up in caring for our boys so that I could have the time to complete this project. To my two beautiful sons, Bobby and Jordan, mommy loves you both very much.

I owe a debt of gratitude to Ms. Marilyn Malcolm for cheering me on and encouraging me along the way. Marilyn was generous enough to read my earlier drafts and provided excellent feedback.

Special thanks to my entire family (Boyd, Bradley, Bankhead, Sears, Chears, Kimble and Crout) especially my mother, Lynette, who raised me on her own. They all are just as excited about this project as I am. I also acknowledge my entire SSA family, especially Matthew Cotton, Debra Cochran, Raymone Hinton, Anjeanette Payton, Angela Barnhart, Nateshia McElroy, Karen Woodson, Denise Anderson, Gloria Cardona, Sandra Peralta, Donna Crawford and Brittani Jefferson.

A very special shout out to my dear grandmother, Mrs. Lula Mae Bradley, who departed this life on July 19, 2015, prior to the completion of this project. She instilled in me endless wisdom and introduced me to God. I am beyond grateful for her. She will FOREVER be in my heart.

It is my sincere hope that Debra's story reaches someone.

This book is dedicated to the loving memory of my dear grandmother, Mrs. Lula Mae Bradley, Dontel, Fred & Novella Morris and Lucas. May they all rest in peace!

Preface

"The mentality and behavior of drug addicts and alcoholics is wholly irrational until you understand that they are completely powerless over their addiction and unless they have structured help, they have no hope."

~Russell Brand

Drug addiction is the all too common and constant culprit of human decay. A wedge that drives families apart and destroys lives. Growing up on the Southside of Chicago and in North Minneapolis, MN, I have become well acquainted with the haunting destruction that drugs leave in its wake. I have witnessed the demise of once successful and well-established individuals who become slaves to the small amount of product that grants temporary moments of glee, while at the same time shattering souls.

Women who were once pretty enough to compete in beauty pageants are reduced to cheap prostitutes willing to do anything to feed their habits, even if it means abandoning their children. Similarly, once respected and revered men transformed into petty thieves willing to rob, steal, or even kill as long as they can get their drugs. This cycle of despair is as common to society as the Chicago wind on a cloudy fall afternoon.

Drug addiction breeds a vicious cycle of broken homes, neglected children, and physical and sexual abuse. In fact, this epidemic is growing more widespread and is spilling over into well-to-do communities. As a child, and even now in my adult life, I often wonder what leads one to turn to drugs. Do people realize how much better their lives can be if they would just get off drugs?

I even took a course on the subject at DePaul University called "Alcoholism, Drug Addiction Recovery" in search of answers and I came to the realization that understanding the beginning of a person's journey is vital and could perhaps lead to answers of said questions. This is how I decided Debra's story needed to be shared. I only knew her as my uncle's skinny girlfriend who talked too much and tried too hard to assert herself into my family. Over time, as I came to know her better, I understood why she was so brash and blunt in her demeanor. It was because she was hurting inside. In fact, I learned Debra experienced a great deal of trauma in her childhood which carried over into her adult life and affected the decisions she made, including her relationship with my uncle.

Among many other things, I wondered why she would allow someone to abuse and mistreat her. I also wondered how this tortured soul came to be so tortured. What was it in her past that made her accept such pain? The great thing about Debra is she freely speaks her mind. She openly shared her life experiences with me, both the good and bad. She was eager to tell her story in hopes of reaching others. Perhaps her story could pull someone back from the brink of drug addiction or give hope to someone struggling to maintain sobriety.

Our goal is to reach lost souls and aid in the eradication of drug addiction and its impact on families and individuals.

Pseudonyms were used to protect the privacy of all individuals involved.

Chapter 1

The room is pitch-black and silent. My body lies across the ice-cold concrete floor. *How did I get down here? Where is everyone? What time of day is it?* I ponder paralyzed by fear.

My face is throbbing and I cannot see out of my left eye. My legs are numb and my head is so heavy it feels as if it will roll away if I try to sit up. The room is spinning as if a tornado is on the horizon. I feel like weeks are passing by as I lie here on this concrete pillow trying to piece together my tumultuous life. For a brief moment I forgot who and where I was. My mind blanks out again, but this time only for a few minutes. I must have really fucked up this time, I think to myself as the room briefly turns pitch-black for a second time. As strength begins to flow back to my body, I begin to gather myself and it all starts coming back to me.

Whish! I see his fists coming at my face like the speed of lightning. His swings were coming so fast I could feel the

ROCK BOTTOM

wind coming off them. My frail frame could not escape them in time. As I bobbed and weaved unsuccessfully, each blow struck my already battered and bruised body like a hammer to a nail. The pain was so excruciating it sent me to the floor in the fetal position. I couldn't catch my breath or gather my bearings enough to attempt to run.

Each time I tried to get up and defend myself he knocked me back down to my knees. I was no match for that giant, especially when he was enraged like that. I decided it was best that I lie there and pray for it to end. I begged him to stop but he was like a man possessed. He kept assaulting me like I was a man on the street who stole his most prized possession. I remember hearing our grandchildren screaming and hollering but there was nothing they could do. I felt ashamed as I could feel them watching from the stairs witnessing the entire scene.

It was awful to hear them pleading, crying, yelling at him, "Granddaddy, please don't kill grandma. Please stop it, granddaddy! Please stop!" They begged.

They witnessed each punch and kick and heard the profanities he spat at me while pouncing on my battered body. Sadly, this was nothing new for them, or me for the matter. These beatings, although not as severe as tonight, occurred often. I am more hurt for them that they had to witness the wickedness of their grandfather than I am for myself.

As I attempted to get up on my feet, I watched him as he picked up the bat from off the floor. I was stuck as stared at the wooden baseball bat coming toward my head - I mentally said goodbye to each of my grandchildren. *Thump!* The sound of the bat making contact with my head. Although it didn't knock me out right away I could still slightly hear the sounds of the children screaming. Their voices rang out to me but it sounded as if I was underwater.

I could hear the muffled sounds of my grandchildren saying, "She's dead! She's dead! She's dead! Grandma's dead!!"

They looked on as my lifeless body crashed to the floor and reality, as I knew it, came to a halt. Visions started to flash in my head and I felt like I was floating on water. I saw myself as a kid again before all of the pain, abuse and abandonment of my life began. My daddy appeared in a bright light, holding my hand telling me everything would be ok. This must be what it feels like to have your life flash before your eyes. I believe this is when I lost consciousness for good because I do not remember anything after that.

I eventually regained consciousness and somehow was able to stumble to my feet off the cold concrete floor. I reached my hands out to feel for the wall. My weakened, broken body clung to the cold, coarse wall as I staggered around it feeling for the light switch. When I turned the light on I saw the horror of what happened to me; however, I could not immediately recall what happened.

The room was a disaster scene like something out of a movie. All of my clothing and other personal items were thrown about. Picture frames were broken and boxes turned over. He even cut up the bedspread that was given to us as a Christmas gift by his oldest daughter. He intentionally destroyed any and everything that meant something to me. I guess whooping my ass wasn't good enough for him.

Of course his belongings were all gone, including the clothes and cologne I just bought him. Like all of the times before when he beat the hell out of me, he would disappear so he wouldn't have to face the black eyes, busted lips, broken noses, or handprints to my face. I have spent many days in the emergency room behind his angry, rage-filled beatings. Each time I declined to press charges because I rationalized his behavior and even blamed myself at times. This time was different because I almost lost my life. I may be a junkie or low class citizen in some peoples' opinions, but I mean something to many people and I'm also a human being who deserves to live life free of abuse and torture.

I noticed a puddle of blood where I laid for what seems like days and I panicked. I remembered the baseball bat coming toward my head and it occurred to me I was hit. No wonder my head was throbbing so badly I thought to myself. I shuffled to the bathroom for the mirror to get a look at the damage. I used my fingers to feel around in my head, it wasn't long before I discovered a knot the size of a golf ball. The area was very tender and all of my hair in that area of my head was matted to my skull from the dried blood.

"Damn!!" I blurted out. "What could I have done to deserve this?" I asked myself even though I already knew the answer. "He was really trying to kill me this time." I uttered staring in the mirror as tears streamed from my yellow-stained eyes and dripped onto the 1993 Chicago Bulls championship t-shirt that was also stained with my blood. Pain and hurt filled my heart as it did so many other times before after the beatings. I felt as if my life did not mean a thing to him as if I wasn't a human being.

He always took his frustrations out on me even though my intentions were always to help. All of his problems were somehow my fault – from the mail carrier delivering his disability check later than usual to the summons for child support. I was to blame for it all.

I slowly began to put the room back together while I wondered which of his women he ran off to be with this time. I grew angrier and angrier with each throb of my head; which helped me to realize the enormity of the situation. He nearly ended my life, took all of the money we had been saving for our own apartment over the past year, and broke everything that meant something to me. He even ripped up my favorite picture of me and my deceased son, Lucas.

Seeing the picture ripped into what seemed like a thousand small pieces sent me into a rage. I could deal with the physical abuse and even him tearing up the few items I held dear to me, but destroying the picture of Lucas and me was my breaking point. I decided that night, there in the dimly light basement, I had enough. I had hit rock bottom and I needed to get clean so that I could take my life back. The drugs lead me to allow him and many others to do whatever they wanted throughout the course of my life. I accepted it all without protest or resistance. For the first time in my life, I was ready to stand up for me and leave behind

all that was hindering the rest of life.

Chapter 2

For years, I threatened to enter rehab and get myself cleaned up so I could move on. This scared him because he knew I would come to my senses and leave him. So his reaction was always to feed me more drugs and string me along with a few weeks of good behavior. Each time I fell right back into his trap believing he was a changed man; only to be disappointed time and time again with more lies, cheating, and beatings.

This was my wake up call. My body was tired of being pummeled, kicked, and spat upon whenever he felt like I needed to be "disciplined" as he called it. I had been using drugs for more than 20 years. It was time for a change. I reflected back over my entire life up until that point - the pain, abuse, and abandonment would all lead to my triumph I declared. I had never expressed myself or dealt with the demons from the past. Instead, drugs were my escape from all of the terrors; it was my therapy, but unfortunately, it offered no real solution. I had accepted abuse from my family members and my ex-husband but none worse than him. I guess God was with me because I am surprised that I survived and was able to talk about it. To reach my destiny I have to start from the beginning so you can understand the full story.

I was born, Debra Marie Morris on October 6, 1954 to James and Mary Pauling at Cook County hospital in Chicago, IL. A lot of my family calls me Debbie I am the oldest of five children, I became a mother long before I had my first child. I cooked, cleaned, washed clothes, fed, and cared for my younger siblings. I acted so much like a mother that my baby sister, Michelle, thought I was her mother. In fact, she called me mama and preferred me over our mother on the rare occasions she attempted to bond with Michelle.

Caring for others came natural to me even at a young age. For as long as I can remember I have always put others ahead of myself. I guess it's because I was never really coddled and loved like most other babies.

My mom was a mom in name only. I don't have many fond memories of her because she spent most of her time running the streets. She would give birth, drop the new baby off at home to me and walk back out the door without explanation. Amazingly, she never suffered any repercussions from being out in the Chicago air before the six-week recovery period was up. I often heard daddy warn her about a set back because she never allowed her body to heal before going back out into the streets. Even during the brutal Chicago winters, she continued to venture out almost immediately after giving birth.

My mother treated pregnancy like a failed attempt at rehab. She would abstain from drugs and alcohol for the first few months, but relapse even worse than before around the second trimester. My baby brother, Derrick, who we call Duck and Michelle were both born with drugs in their blood stream. Mama left the hospital with both of them before the Department of Children and Family Services could be notified. They each went through long, uncontrollable crying spells throughout the day and night during the first few months of their lives. I often overheard the grown folks say that the babies were suffering from withdrawal because of the drugs mama took during her pregnancy.

I always knew when mama was high off drugs because she would sit on the couch and stare up at the ceiling like she was watching the greatest movie ever made. Then every once in a while she would abruptly get up and look out the window. During these times she was quiet and aloof. We knew better than to bother her with our presence because she could be unpredictable. Once the high was over she turned back into the vicious, uncaring, and mean individual we knew her to be.

One time I asked mama why she often stayed away from us for days at a time. Then I repeated a comment that I overheard from my aunt Carmen, daddy's sister, about kids, especially girls, needing their mother. Before I could fully get the words out of my mouth, she was on top of me, hitting and yelling obscenities. I could smell the liquor on her breath. Daddy had to pull her off me. I learned then not to question her about anything. She did not answer to anyone, including my father.

My daddy did what he could for us but he had his own issues being a functional alcoholic. He drove a cab by night, and occasionally during the day, and spent the daytime sleeping off his hangovers. For the most part we had to fend for ourselves. Every first of the month my mother would go grocery shopping for just enough food to last us until the next month's food stamps arrived. We ate a lot of canned goods, boxed foods and ramen noodles - the cheapest items in the store.

Daddy made sure the rent and other bills were paid, but there was rarely enough money left over to buy clothes, shoes, or personal hygiene items. I hated going to school, I was teased every day because my clothes were too little and had holes, my hair was rarely combed and I had bad teeth. The kids even sang songs about me, "Payless shoes ain't got no grip, you gone fall and bust your lip" was their favorite.

On top of that, I was always in special education classes. I found it funny how other kids that were also in special education classes made me the butt of their jokes. Most of them were on the same level as me - dumb when it came to schoolwork and living in poverty. To this day, I still cannot read or write like most other adults. I have never read a book from beginning to end. To make up for this I had great street smarts which I consider to be a blessing from God. Having street smarts proved to be more valuable to me than any book could have ever been. Nobody on the streets cares about how many books you have read or how high you scored on tests.

By the time I got to fourth grade, I stopped going to school on a regular basis. I would miss days at a time and nobody noticed. By then mom had disappeared and left us with daddy when she found a new man named Greg. Unfortunately for us Greg did not want any kids, so momma left us behind without a second thought. After a few months, she returned without explanation. Daddy welcomed her back with open arms. Not only because he struggled to care for us on his own but also because he loved her deeply. She did not feel for daddy the way he felt for her.

No matter how many times she left us or boldly declared their marriage and us kids were a mistake, he always accepted her back with open arms. In fact, he never spoke a bad word about her even though she treated him, and us, like shit. When I think back on their relationship I am convinced she is what drove daddy to drink. Despite his alcoholism he was a good man, especially to his children.

He came home to us every night, made sure we knew he loved us, and brought his money home. He loved to drink but it never interfered with our well-being or livelihood. He did what he could with the limited resources he had but we needed our mother. We did not have anyone to nurse us when we fell ill or felt bad about ourselves. On the rare occasion mama was home we knew not to bother her. She usually wanted to rest for a couple of days then we would not see her again for weeks at a time.

We actually preferred for her to stay away because her presence changed the dynamic of the household. When mama was home we walked on eggshells and had to be quiet all the time. We could not play any of our made up games or watch TV. We often had to find ways to amuse ourselves and pass the time because we did not have any toys and weren't allowed to go outside. At times, we would sit in the window of our third floor apartment and look down at the people passing by. On occasion, we found humor in cursing out the hookers and pimps that conducted business in front of our building. We knew they could not get to us and most of the time daddy was sleeping off his hangover. He never found out.

One weekend daddy's baby brother, June, came to stay with us after his wife, Joanne, put him out. This would happen from time to time because he liked to drink too, but unlike daddy, he could be very unpleasant when he got drunk. Uncle June was a lot of fun to us, we were always happy to see him. He played with us, told funny stories and showed us a lot of love. He was the only one of all my relatives, other than daddy, to ever utter the words, "I love you." Although he was often drunk when he spattered it, I always believed the words, "Uncle loves you", came straight from his heart. Daddy's family was more loving and caring compared to mama's side. Uncle June spent the most time around us because he was close with daddy. He always came with gifts or he would buy us McDonald's, which was a luxury in those days.

Uncle June and daddy drank heavily the entire weekend. Daddy's favorite drink was Wild Irish Rose because he could get a lot of liquor for a low cost; and every corner store in our neighborhood kept it in full stock. Uncle June eventually passed out on the floor near the couch where daddy laid, his long legs dangled off the edge.

I watched as daddy drank an entire bottle in one sitting. I noticed that his hands began to swell up and his speech became more slurred than usual as he called for us to go to bed. He then staggered from the raggedy, blue-suede couch that was just off the kitchen, his heavy boots dragged on the worn out carpet as he made his way to the bedroom. Along the way, he bumped his thigh on the sharp edge of the coffee table but there was no reaction. He walked like one of the zombies from the *Night of the Living Dead*. His body hit the bed with a loud thud! Soon his eyes were lifeless and his body lay limp.

Briefly after, all we could hear was daddy's loud snoring. He was so loud it drowned out the sound of the hoods playing dice in our hallway. Saturday nights were always very rowdy in our building, especially around the first of the month when most people received their welfare and/or SSI checks.

I did not sleep well that night. I was in and out of my sleep with anxiety but I did not know why. The next morning, I tried to wake daddy for work, as he had taken a morning shift that Sunday, but I knew instantly something was terribly wrong. His hands were heavy, ice cold, and claylike. I screamed, pinched, pushed and pulled at his body but he would not respond. One of his arms felt as if it weighed more than my entire body. After a while I directed my little brother, Duck, to go into the kitchen for a cold glass of water to pour in daddy's face. I had seen someone do that on TV before. Unfortunately, it did not work. He continued to lay there with his eyes and mouth partially open. When he did not respond Duck went into a frenzy, screaming and hollering, "Daddy is dead. Debbie, daddy is dead!!"

It was then I noticed he was not breathing because his chest was not moving up and down. To be sure I put my hand underneath his nose but there was no air. Then it hit me, my daddy really was dead.

Uncle June overhearing the commotion jumped up out of his sleep and went straight to daddy. I watched in shock as Uncle June pushed on daddy's chest then he frantically tried breathing air into his mouth. He was shaking so badly I thought he would pass out. After several minutes and numerous attempts daddy still would not budge.

Out of what seemed like desperation, Uncle June collapsed onto daddy's chest sobbing loudly, "Get up, James!" He demanded. "You have to go to work, man. Get up! You got these kids here, man! They need you, man!!" He pleaded.

We all stood there and watched as Uncle June tried to hide the fear written all over his face. At this point, he began to come to grips with the reality that his best friend, his brother was dead. This was evident because I had only seen Uncle June this emotional on one other occasion, when Grandma Hazel died. I was 5 years old and too young then to understand how her passing would affect our lives. He tugged at daddy's arms a few more times as if he thought daddy would magically wake up out of a drunken stupor. Daddy had a history of blacking out for several hours at a time after drinking heavily. I knew that was not the case this time around. Slowly Uncle Joe regained his composure, wiped his tears and ordered us kids to go into our bedroom and close the door.

We did not have a phone in our apartment so Uncle Joe went next door to Miss Emma's to call the paramedics. He paced the floor for what seemed like hours waiting for them to arrive. We lived in a rough part of Chicago so the police never showed up right away; there were some occasions when they did not show up at all. I watched the clock and counted in silence as the thirty-five minutes crawled by. The fire department as usual was the first to arrive. I couldn't help but wonder what took so long considering the fire station was just down the block.

We peeked through the key hole of the bedroom door as the scary looking men hurriedly filed in one-by-one asking Uncle June question after question. Daddy's stiff body laid still with his eyes gazing up at the ceiling and his mouth hanging wide open revealing his crooked teeth. They cut open his white V-neck t-shirt and pumped on his chest some more. Then they hooked him up to some defibrillator machine and placed two controllers on his chest. Each time they placed the controllers on his chest daddy's body jerked violently. Still he would not respond even after one of the men massaged daddy's chest.

Then one of the men said to the other, "Time of death between 3am and 6am."

Uncle June sat near the dining room window that allow a view into daddy's bedroom. He sat motionless with his arms folded across his chest observing the whole scene. He appeared to be in a state of shock. Then he collapsed to the floor when daddy's death was officially announced. He laid there on the floor for a while sobbing like a newborn baby, staring up at the sky as if he were waiting for daddy to appear.

Then suddenly the room fell silent, as he appeared to be deep in thought about what to do next. He appeared to contemplate how to move on with life without his best friend. Daddy being the oldest always protected Uncle June. Whenever he was in trouble or needed advice he sought out daddy. June always came to visit daddy and the two of them would carry on reminiscing about their childhood and "the good ole days" as they called it. Neither daddy nor June had many friends because they had each other, especially after their parents died.

The whole scene was so surreal, I felt as if I were in a bad dream that I could not wake up from. I hoped it was a dream so that I would not have to admit to seeing the paramedics wheel my father out of our dingy apartment wrapped in a white sheet. I wished I didn't have to witness the white paramedics' feeble attempts at performing mouth-to-mouth resuscitation on a poor, alcoholic, dead Black man or the medical wrappings strewn about the floor of daddy's bedroom. Nor did I wish to see my favorite uncle balled up on the floor sobbing uncontrollably like a newborn baby longing for his mother. Uncle June was inconsolable.

I felt helpless because I did not know how to fix it. Thoughts of what to do raced through my mind. I wanted to go to Uncle June and tell him everything would be ok somehow. My legs were feeling heavy like lead and prevented me from moving. My mind rapidly replayed scenes from my happiest moments with daddy, such as my ninth birthday when he surprised me with a new coat. I also thought about our last Christmas together when he gave me a brand new baby doll still in the packaging. Daddy always found ways to make Christmas and our birthdays special. Thinking of him in this way made me smile even though my heart and soul was hurting.

Now he would be gone forever which left me with a profound feeling of sadness, especially once I realized we would be left alone to struggle in the cruel world. This made me feel so nauseous I thought I would vomit all over the floor. Then I somehow gathered the strength to go to Uncle June and helped him snap out of his trance.

Raising his head to face me, the look in his eyes told me that life would never be the same again for him. He mouthed to me, "I am here for you, baby girl", while his blood shot eyes searched my face for emotion. I was devastated inside but my external toughness would not allow me to cry or fall apart in the presence of others. Life with mama forced me to be strong beyond my ten years of life. I understood that others were watching me so I had to keep it together so they would not fall apart.

Lost in his sorrow Uncle June left us alone in the apartment so he could make phone calls to inform the family. We all watched out the living room window as he made his way across the street to the pay phone on the corner. Even in his walk, I could tell he was hurting badly inside. His wide hips slowly swayed with the breezy October wind. From the window we stared in silence as he buried his face in his hands leaning against the rusty phone booth door. I knew Uncle June was not in his right mind because on any other day he would not have stood in that small space for any amount of time to inhale the strong stench of urine and no telling what else.

Tears flowed from his as he rocked back and forth in the small booth while sobbing loudly into the phone. He kept putting his head in his hands and shaking his head. He smoked cigarette after cigarette as he dialed multiple numbers on the phone. Meanwhile people from the neighborhood paced around the booth staring at Uncle June trying to figure out why he was crying.

Soon the intrigue of it all wore off and my brothers and sisters began roaming about the apartment as they usually did on Sunday mornings. They laughed, giggled and played as I struggled to keep my emotions in check so that tears would not stream down my face. I knew if I started to cry I would not be able to stop the tears from flowing.

My mind wandered about what to do next as Uncle June slowly made his way back toward our building. Even though he was the adult in this situation, I felt the weight of everything on my shoulders because I understood what was to come. I knew that our future was uncertain because the only person who cared about us was now gone forever. We did not know where our next meal would come from let alone who would take us in. The stress of it all was a blessing in disguise - I was too preoccupied contemplating our future to cry.

Chapter 3

"Who's going to take care of us now, Uncle June?" I asked as he walked through the door.

By now he seemed to have regained his composure, taking my hands into his he sat me down and explained. "Baby girl, we are going to find your mom. When she finds out what has happened she will be here. She loves all of you. Everything is going to be ok, sweetheart." He said looking away. Even he did not believe that crock of bullshit.

He knew mama well enough to know she was not going to suddenly give up her crack addiction and her love of freedom to be tied down in the house with a bunch of kids - even if they were her own. I could still smell the Wild Irish Rose seeping from his pores so I assumed he was still drunk from the night before.

"But Uncle June!" I quickly shot back. "Mama don't love us like daddy. She never comes home!" I moaned putting my head down.

"Listen here, Debbie, your mama is just going through a tough time right now. Everything will get better with time." He said rubbing his giant mechanic hands through my long, curly, untamed hair. I could smell the odor of motor oil on top of Wild Irish Rose as he pulled his hands away.

"You don't understand!" I continued. "Mama doesn't come home for days at a time. We are always here alone..."

Cutting me off he took my hands into his own again, "Listen to me, Debbie, your mama is a good lady. She loves all of you kids. Trust me, she will be here for you kids now that your daddy is gone." He said not even looking me in the face.

I was hoping he would take us to live with him and his wife, Joanne. Although she could be evil at times, she was always nice and friendly with us. She had a tendency to speak her mind and say things out loud that others were thinking in their head. Most of the family did not like how outspoken she was but I liked her. She could also be very stern and had no problem with spanking kids who "don't mind adults" as she would say.

28

I even considered how beneficial our living with them would be for Uncle June. I thought maybe she would not be so quick to put him out for every one of his many indiscretions. She often threatened to divorce him and take half of everything he owned, which wasn't much. He liked to drink just like daddy and he spent much of what he earned on booze. Because of his drinking, she would always say to him, "We ain't Siamese twins. You get a lawyer and I will get me one." I always wondered why she wouldn't save herself the trouble and leave him if he made her that unhappy, especially since they did not have any children together.

Without warning, mama came bursting through the front door like a mad woman on a mission just as I was about to beg Uncle June to take us all to live with him.

"Where's James? Where is he, Junie?" She asked. Her voice cracking as scant tears streamed down her dirty face. Word of daddy's sudden passing reached her somehow. People in the neighborhood reported everything that went on in our apartment at 738 W. 69th St. to mama.

Judging by her appearance and mannerisms, I could tell she was still high off drugs. Knowing her in the ways I did I was sure she took a few hits off the pipe before coming home. Her lips were twitching, hair standing straight up, eyes bulging, and she smelled bad. These were all signs my mama was a total junkie and I was ashamed of her.

Uncle June wrapped his long arms around her tiny waist and held her like she was a toddler. He did not seem to be bothered by her poor appearance, the god-awful stench, nor her fake cries. I watched in disgust as she cried out, "James, I love you, baby! Please come back to us. We need you!"

Through all of her screams and cries only a few tears managed to fall from her bulging eyes. Then Uncle June began to cry all over again but his tears were genuine. I did not doubt his love for daddy. He kept saying to her, "You have to be strong for the kids, Mary. They are going to need you." She continued to sob even louder without any tears falling.

My siblings continued to play in the next room and I sat there wondering about life with mama. After a few more minutes of her Oscar-worthy performance she motioned for me to come to her. I slowly walked in her direction with my head down debating the whole way how I should react. Her last interaction with daddy was not a pleasant one. I replayed it in my mind over and over again. I was surprised when she put her arms out to hug me. I had never shared a warm and emotional moment with her in all my ten years of life. Needless to say, the moment was very awkward for me.

I decided not to hug her back because I was convinced she did not deserve my love. It felt strange to hear her utter to me, "We gone make it, Debbie. We are going to be alright. Mama is here, baby." She sobbed into my ear.

I searched her face to be sure this woman was the Mary Pauling I had known. I could not believe those words were coming from her mouth. The whole exchange was weird and I could not wait for it to be over.

Daddy's funeral was held five days later at Gatling's funeral home. In the days leading up to his funeral I felt strong as I continued to remind myself that he was now my own personal guardian angel. I handled everything well until the night before when I realized I would never see him again after the funeral. The mere thought of continuing on in life without him made me sick to the point of vomiting. For the first time since his death, I allowed myself to cry as I pondered how I would say goodbye. Every time I closed my eyes, I saw daddy laying there in the bed with his eyes and mouth half open, tongue sticking out. I could still feel his cold claylike skin touching me. My daddy was gone forever and I had to figure out how to accept that.

My first time ever seeing daddy in a suit was him resting peacefully in a casket with his eyes closed as if he were fast asleep. He no longer had to stress himself worrying about where mama was, whom she was with, or how he would feed us. I believe daddy drank because he loved alcohol, the friend he hoped would mend his broken heart. Mama was his first love and he was proud of that fact;

even though momma was ashamed of his dark skin, the

beer gut he gained over the years and the fact that he drove

a cab. She always reminded him of how he ruined her life.

Still he always tried his best to please her but nothing was

ever good enough.

Chapter 4

Soon after the funeral services were over she began to ransack the apartment looking for any money he may have stashed away. Daddy did not have any money hidden but she found his prized coin collection grandpa had left for him. Daddy was very proud of the family heirloom that was passed down to him. He felt special because grandpa left it for him instead of Uncle June. From time to time he would polish the coins and tell us about grandpa and his love of them. He loved to reminisce about old times.

I was sad to see mama ease out of the backdoor with the wooden case grandpa handcrafted himself. I knew we would never see that case or coins again. Several weeks later she received a check from the Social Security Administration. The check must have been for a large amount of money because she was in a good mood after opening the envelope. Then she disappeared for longer than the usual two to three days.

After the fourth day, I decided to do something because we did not have any food in the apartment and Michelle was out of baby milk. We gave her sugar water for as long as we could but eventually that no longer pacified her. She also had been running a fever and had diarrhea. I later learned this was because her teeth were starting to come in.

Desperate, I sent Duck around the corner to momma's friend, Cookie's house but there was no sign of her there. Duck tried a few more of her hangouts but no one saw her or knew where she was. With no signs of hope, I decided that Duck and I would have to panhandle for at least a can of milk for Michelle. I figured the rest of us would have to suffer a little while longer.

So we stood on the corner of the A&P Deli and begged strangers for money as they exited the store, telling them our mama was sick and we needed money for food. This was actually a fair statement come to think about it. To our surprise, we collected more than $10.00 within minutes.

This was a small fortune to us considering we did not have any food in the house. I was able to buy Michelle a can of baby milk and us a pack of hot dogs, a loaf of bread, a small bottle of ketchup, and a two liter of Nehi pop. I even had a small amount of change left over which I decided to keep in case we needed something else later on.

This turned out to be a good decision because another three days passed and mama still had not come home and nobody knew where she was. Michelle was crying again and the hot dogs and bread were gone. Duck and I went back to the A&P Deli to beg for money again, naively thinking we would collect another $10.00. This time was different because majority of the customers remembered us from days before and our sob story about mama being sick and us being hungry did not work as well. We collected a few coins but not nearly enough to buy Michelle's milk and get us something to eat.

I thought about stealing the baby milk and some lunchmeat for us but I quickly decided against that plan realizing our faces well known at the A&P Deli and other stores in the neighborhood. Besides, they always watched us very closely whenever we entered the store even if mama was with us. Remembering a conversation I overheard between mama and her friend, Cookie, I thought of another plan.

Cookie worked as a cashier at the A&P Deli for a short time until they discovered she was stealing more money than she was taking in. She always complained to mama about the owner, Mr. Parker, throwing away hot food he was unable to sell. They also discarded canned and boxed foods and other items past the expiration date. Our next plan would be to dumpster dive for the hot food and other discarded items after the store closed each night.

This would be easy because we only lived about a block away and we could grab the food while it was still hot. Because we could not distinguish our building from the others on our street we put an empty easy bake oven box in the back bedroom window so that we could know where home was.

Every night for about a week, we waited for Mr.

Parker to set the black bag inside the large garbage can

before we made our move. I would climb inside and Duck

would be the lookout. We carried out our plan without a hitch

for several nights. Then on about the fourth night as we

approached the back of the store, we noticed two brown

paper bags full of hot food sitting on top of the garbage can.

Through a small crack in the back door window I could see

Mr. Parker's bulky silhouette staring out the window,

watching as we quickly grabbed the bags and started back

down the dark alley.

We followed this same routine for the next several

nights without any interruptions. The bags were always

there at closing time and Mr. Parker even added canned

pops and candy. Then one night I noticed his shadow in the

darkness following us up the alley. He stayed a safe

distance behind and watched as we entered through the

back door of our run down building. He was still standing

there as I removed the easy bake oven box from the

window. After a few moments, he started back down the alley toward the store.

As we got ready for bed that night, we heard a loud husky voice on the other end of our front door yelling, "Police!" Then he violently banged on our door. We all scattered in our apartment like the roaches did whenever the lights came on. I took Michelle, hid her tiny body inside one of the raggedy dresser drawers and closed it. Then I climbed underneath the folding couch we all slept on at night. The others hid in the hall closet underneath a large pile of our dirty clothes.

When nobody came to the door, the police broke it down. Before long, our tiny apartment was swarming with burly police officers yelling out to us as they mishandled our already mangled furniture looking for us. When it became apparent the apartment was empty I heard them preparing to leave, one whispered to the other, "That old man doesn't know what the hell he's talking about. There ain't nobody here".

The noise of it all and being confined in that dresser must have gotten to Michelle because she suddenly started to scream and holler. Her muffled cries got louder and louder as the men shuffled around the room trying to decipher where the noise was coming from. Realizing they were on to us we all emerged from our hiding places.

In some ways I was relieved we no longer had to be alone. The weather was cold outside and we did not have any heat. Nights were the worse, not only because of the drunks and crackheads arguing in the hallway, but also because we were afraid. The darkness scared the little ones and every creek of the floor put me on edge. I did not sleep well at night out of fear of someone coming in on us.

I later learned Mr. Parker contacted the Department of Children and Family Services and the police because he feared we were alone. After he watched us remove the easy bake oven box from the window, he was convinced there were no adults around to look after us. The police officers questioned each of us about the whereabouts of our mother and father. When it became apparent we were in fact alone they removed us all from the apartment. We didn't even have time to scrounge up any of our clothes or the few toys we had.

We were sent to live with my mother's oldest brother, Maurice and his family because he had space for the five of us. I begged and pleaded with the social worker to send us to Uncle June's house but she would not listen. I have always believed they put us off on the first relative to answer the phone that night.

Uncle Maurice and his wife, Wanda, came to rescue us in the wee hours of the morning. They loaded us into their brand new station wagon and drove in silence to the big blue house they called home. They lived in a much better neighborhood than we did. I could tell he was not happy about taking us in. As he was unloading the car I heard him whisper to Wanda with a look of scorn and regret on his face, "How did we get stuck with five damn kids?"

I could understand his frustration because he did not know much about any of us. We did not have much of a relationship with any of mama's relatives because she rarely took us around them. She never really took us anywhere not even for regular medical checkups. The state had to threaten to remove us from the home before she took us to be vaccinated each school year.

Mama was the black sheep of her family, meaning she caused the most trouble. Of her seven brothers and sisters, she turned out to be the worse, even when compared to Uncle Pee Wee who spent time in jail throughout the 1970s and 80s for selling drugs, burglary and writing bad checks. Whenever she had the chance, Grandma Gloria reminded mama about her many childhood indiscretions no matter who was around. She would intentionally embarrass mama in front of people in the neighborhood as often as she could.

Somehow, the subject always turned to drugs and alcohol when mama was around. If mama wasn't being demeaned for having the most kids in the family, she was criticized for the way she looked, dressed, and talked. Not only was mama criticized but we were referred to as ugly, nappy-headed and many other things. Daddy was not excluded from Grandma Gloria's wrath. She and the rest of the family disliked daddy and they did not make a secret of it. They never had any kind words to say about him.

Daddy was not welcome in Grandma's house under any circumstance, not even when mama's oldest sister Sarah, died. Despite their hate for him, daddy was always respectful of them and would have been more than willing to welcome any of them into our shabby apartment. Daddy encouraged mama to spend more time with her family, especially Grandma Gloria as she began to grow older and her health started to deteriorate. Mama was adamant about staying away from her family unless someone died. Even then, she would pay her respects but refused to stick around for any repast events. Mama's one true act of loyalty and kindness toward daddy was staying away from her family because of how they felt about us and him.

From the time we arrived at Maurice and Wanda's home it was obvious she did not love us in the same way she did her other grandchildren. She adored Maurice's kids, especially his oldest son, Vance, whom we all knew was her pick. Mama always referred to Vance as the golden boy because he could do no wrong. He was supposedly well behaved and always got good grades in school. He was the model of a good kid, something Grandma Gloria told us we should all aspire to be. Vance was heavily praised for even the most trivial acts, like saying, please and thank you.

Even though we were looked down upon we all had good manners, thanks to daddy. He taught us to respect our elders and each other. We were not bad kids. In fact, we were well behaved and looked after each other because we were so accustomed to being on our own. Still, we were talked about and picked on for every little thing we did. Unlike Vance, we could never use our age as an excuse for making a mistake. On occasion Vance would misbehave in school, sass adults, and would steal money from his parents. Grandma and the others always excused his behavior and brushed it off saying he "will grow out of it."

Now I understood why mama occasionally sat off to herself in a corner drinking beer, listening to old songs on the radio, and rambled to herself about how badly she was treated growing up. During these times I felt badly for her because she seemed like a lost soul who was ready to give up on life. I convinced myself that she could not love daddy or us because she did not know how to love. Grandma Gloria loved mama because she had to but not because she wanted to.

Mama's family never contacted us on holidays, our birthdays, or checked in with us - I believed it was because they never really cared about us. Given her strained history with the family, I thought she would fight to get us back. Instead, we did not have any contact with her whatsoever for nearly a year. She did not visit us or even attempt to find out how we were doing. This was an assumption because Uncle Maurice never mentioned it. Mama probably was happy to finally be rid of us, I thought to myself.

She knew her brother did not care much for us. Besides, he had a family of his own. Listening to the grown - ups talk, I found out he decided to take custody of us only after learning he would receive cash and food stamp benefits from the state each month. Daddy had only been in the ground for two months and our lives were already in shambles.

Chapter 5

Uneasiness fell over me immediately after moving into Uncle Maurice's house. I did not care much for Vance, not only because he was the chosen one, but also because he gave me strange looks. I didn't feel comfortable being alone with him for any length of time because I did not feel he could be trusted. I found it odd that a teenage boy preferred to spend so much time around younger kids, especially girls. He never really spent any time with kids his own age doing teenage activities.

Even during the summer months when the neighborhood boys gathered to play sports, go bike riding, or play the dozen he was never interested. Instead, he hung around the house with the grown-ups watching soap operas and gossiping about people from the neighborhood. I grew concerned when he took a particular interest in me and consistently found reasons to be in our area of the house.

The five of us shared a small bedroom with an adjoining bathroom at the back of the house.

It did not take long for me to figure out why Vance liked being around me and the reason for the strange looks. Within a week of our arrival the sexual abuse against me started. He would sneak into our room at night, guide me through the darkness to the basement and have his way with me. Sometimes he would tie my tiny hands behind my back, stuff a sock in my mouth and force himself inside me from behind. I was forced to perform oral sex on him nearly every day. He was always rough with me and used demeaning language.

The first time I bled for three days but I didn't think about telling anyone because I knew better. Fearing someone would find out I made sure to thoroughly clean myself up as best I could after each violation. When I could not clean the blood out of my panties I would throw them away. No one ever noticed me sneaking out to the garbage can late at night, my underwear disappearing, or my solemn demeanor as I battled the anger raging inside of me. I became withdrawn and stayed to myself. My behavior went unquestioned.

Fearing I might tell one of the adults in the family about the abuse, Vance threatened to have us all put into foster care if I told anyone. I understood foster care meant we would be separated and I did not want that. I also understood telling the adults was not an option because they would never take my word over his. So I decided to get him in another way, by resisting.

I often had bruises covering both arms and legs, which I blamed on my tendency to be clumsy. No one ever questioned why I was so clumsy or how my clumsiness led to so many bruises. Eventually I decided it would be best to lay there and deal with it.

I trained myself to block it all out - his bad body odor, bad breath, and his sick enjoyment of it all. My mind would drift off to another world where I and my brothers and sisters were kings and queens. I daydreamed about my father coming back to life so he could save us. In my fairytale world, we lived in a huge mansion in the Hollywood Hills. We had maids for cleaning, security guards for protection, and chefs to prepare world class meals. Daddy had also taught me about God, so I prayed a lot, asking him to save us.

All of my praying eventually paid off because out of the blue mama came back for us. Although I knew life with mama would not be much better, I wanted the abuse to stop particularly because Vance was starting to give my six-year-old sister, Janet, the same strange looks he had given me. This terrified me because I knew what he was capable of and I would not be able to stop him.

I had never been so happy to see mama than the day she showed up to Uncle Maurice's demanding for him to release her "goddamn kids." Without so much as a whisper in objection Uncle Maurice and Wanda quickly gathered our things and sent us to be with mama. He seemed to be a little saddened to see us go but still he did not object. I was not sure if it was the money he would miss or the guilt over how we were treated that led to his obvious sadness. He gave each of us a hug as we exited the large house we had come to know as home. Grandma Gloria stayed in her room and did not bother to say a peep to any of us.

We then stepped back into the unknown with mama causing me to feel conflicted. God had finally answered my prayers, but I was not sure I was ready to be back with mama. Even though I endured sexual abuse for the better part of a year and constant pettiness from Grandma Gloria, having a good meal each night and stable shelter meant everything to me. As the oldest child, I functioned as a parent to my younger siblings. I watched over and protected them. I got up at night to feed Michelle and played doctor when any of them became ill. I learned how to comb hair and looked after them as best I could. I managed to develop a routine and became accustomed to life with mama's family.

I was extremely nervous during the entire ride from Uncle Maurice's big, pretty house in a good neighborhood to mama's shabby apartment back on the low end of the city. I watched out the window as the raggedy station wagon seemed to hit every bump and pot hole in the road. I noticed how the people and homes went from bright and sunny with green, manicured lawns to dirt patches for grass and blocks of old, ugly gray buildings that were all identical.

My stomach sank when the station wagon came to a screeching halt in front of what looked like an abandoned building. This one looked even worse than the one we were rescued from nearly a year earlier. There were several people sitting outside on the steps, drinking beer, playing loud music, and over talking one another. She ushered us from the station wagon to her third floor apartment. A strong stench of urine met us at the door, which let me know not much had changed with mama. She was still allowing herself to become so intoxicated and high off drugs that she would unknowingly piss herself.

It was not uncommon for her to go days at a time without changing her clothes or bathing whenever she was on a binge, which could last for weeks at a time. Mama cared more about drinking and using drugs than she did us. She was never warm or loving toward us. In fact, most of the time, she was too drunk or high to tend to her motherly duties. I was convinced her motivation to come for us had everything to do with the financial assistance the State and Social Security provided rather than her love for us.

The apartment was dark and damp with very few windows. There were four bedrooms each with mattresses sprawled across the wooden floors, newspaper covering all the windows of the apartment, a few pieces of old worn down furniture decorated the living room, and mama had one small TV in her room. Within minutes of being there I wanted to scream because I missed the cleanliness and fresh smell of flowers at Uncle Maurice's house. However, I did not miss the abuse – again, I felt conflicted.

Mama introduced the man who accompanied us as Mr. Willie, he was her new friend. After a few days it was obvious to me she had moved on from daddy. Now he was a distant memory that could only live on in my heart. In the beginning, Mr. Willie seemed to be a nice man who kept quiet and stayed to himself. He did not seem to be bothered by the loud noise or Michelle's outburst throughout the night that seemed to keep us all awake, especially me. Nor did Duck's whimpers from nightmares during the night bother him.

He never had much to say to us kids. He stayed locked up in the bedroom all day only coming out for a bathroom break or a trip to the refrigerator every hour or so for a beer. Mama went out of her way to make sure the refrigerator was always stocked with his favorite beer, Schlitz Malt Liquor. I could never understand how she managed to keep the refrigerator stocked with beer when Duck and I had to steal or panhandle for food.

Vance made me question every male in my life. I assumed they were all the same, all after the same thing, sex. Thankfully, Mr. Willie never bothered me in that way but after a while, he changed for the worst. Suddenly everything we did or said got on his nerves.

First, Mr. Willie encouraged mama to beat us for everything, big or small and she happily complied without hesitation. When he learned about Duck's habit of wetting

the bed, he beat him nearly every day. Mr. Willie made the
rest of us watch as he made Duck strip and repeatedly hit
his bare behind with a belt. This was supposed to serve as a
warning for the rest us to behave or suffer the same fate as
Duck. We did not know at the time but these beating would
go on to haunt Duck for the rest of his life.

Mama became a target of his beatings, too, but that
did not bother us in the least bit. I figured it was pay back for
the way she treated us and allowed us to be treated.

We were rescued from Mr. Willie when he tried to pull
the wool over the eyes of the wrong drug dealer. He became
known for passing off fake money when buying his drugs.
After getting away with it several times he began to brag to
his friends about it. Before long the word got out and he was
beaten to death.

No sooner than Mr. Willie's old, decrepit looking body
was buried in the cemetery on Fairfield, mama was
introducing us to another man. She bounced from man to
man without discrimination. She liked them young, old, big,

tall, fat or ugly - it did not matter. They all had one thing in common, addiction to either heroin or crack cocaine. Her sole reason for living seemed to be dedicated to keeping the neighborhood drug dealers rich. She gave them every penny that ever hit her hands.

Mama was one of the most valued customers so she often got drugs on credit when she did not have any money. The dealers would make their rounds throughout our building every first of the month. They made sure to get there before the landlord came around to collect rent. Each month I listened to mama stutter and stammer through lies to our landlord, Mr. Jones about why the rent would be late. Mr. Jones was a nice old man so he took her lame excuses month after month. He knew mama was a drug addict but he felt sorry for us kids.

Eventually Mr. Jones' sympathy wore off because he taped a yellow eviction notice to our door when she missed two consecutive months of paying rent. He told mama she could no longer take advantage of his kind heart. Somehow, she came up with the money to avoid eviction but we were in the same predicament a few months later. She always owed money to multiple people so she never had anything left over after her debts were paid. Soon she resorted to stealing and prostitution to finance her habit.

One after the other, strange men took turns with her in our apartment. The funny noises, slapping sounds, and her skimpy clothes complete with lopsided wigs were all clues about her work. On the rare occasion when I attended school, the other kids found ways to torment me. From me being in special education classes to the chants of "Debbie's mama is a crack hoe." The kids got great enjoyment out of teasing me, especially since I was not the type to fight back. I internalized it all and let it out whenever I had a quiet moment alone.

I continued to amazing me how most of them were in the same special education classes with me and their mothers, too, were crack whores who hung out with my mother. We were all poor and most of our parents were messed up parents, yet, I was the target for the bullying. At night, I often talked to God and cried. I mostly cried because I missed my daddy and I wanted a better life for us. I hurt inside for myself, my siblings, and even mama. I often wondered about the thoughts floating inside her head and why she did not want a better life for herself and us.

Mama's lifestyle was no secret to anyone especially the men in the area. I saw ministers, shop owners, and even drug dealers enter and leave our apartment. Any man that came to our apartment was there for one reason, mama's service. She gained the nickname "Jawbone" because of how good she was at providing oral sex. Men could not get enough of how she made them feel. One thing is for certain, she never lacked for customers.

Chapter 6

Friday nights were always busy for mama. Some men would spend their entire paychecks with her. I could always tell who they were by the way they slowly took their walk of shame down the alley, head down, mumbling to themselves as if formulating a story to tell their significant others how their entire paycheck disappeared within a matter of hours.

In the years after my father's death, we never had any form of stability except the year we spent with Uncle Maurice and his family. We moved from one shabby building to the next on the low end of Chicago because mama could never keep the rent paid, despite all of the men she was servicing. Each apartment was worse than the last because landlords learned not to rent to mama. The ones that took a chance were referred to as "slumlords" who were known for renting to anybody without references or investigating rental history. We often lived without lights and survived the brutal Chicago winters without heat or hot water.

Then my whole life changed when I met my future husband, Charles. I met Charles at the bus stop one cold, blustery, winter morning on one of the rare occasions I decided to attend school. Mama required me to attend school at least two or three days out of each month, so she could keep her public aid benefits. I had seen him a few times before but we never exchanged words just nervous glances in each other's direction, occasionally meeting eyes. He was two years ahead of me and appeared to come from the same type of broken environment as me. His mom was like mine, a drug addict who lived more for drugs than she did for her kids.

Wavy black hair laid perfectly on top of his peanut shaped head. His dark brown eyes gleamed of innocence as he looked in my direction. We exchanged a brief glance and he shot me a quick smile revealing his pearly white teeth. His thin pink lips sat perfectly on his round face. An old scar resembling a small spider rested across the center of his forehead.

There was something appealing about him. Perhaps it was his caramel colored skin or his slender build. I found him to be attractive even though he was short. I saw a soothing comfort in his eyes. A comfort I had never experienced before and something in his smile sent jitterbugs throughout my stomach, which made me nervous.

He talked with a bit of a lisp but he had a free spirit about him. I watched as he interacted with the other kids on the bus stop. He was always loud, cracking jokes and talking shit. I could tell the others looked up to him. He was one of the cool kids so I could not understand why he was making eyes with me. I wanted to be seen and not heard. I managed to fly under the radar and hid in crowds. I never wanted to draw attention to myself.

I was shocked when he approached me that morning, asking my name and where I lived. He ran in the same circle as my little brother, Duck - who by now was a ranking leader of a local gang and was selling drugs. Duck was well-known in our neighborhood and others feared him. We did not have to worry about anyone bothering us because everyone knew Duck was our brother.

Duck developed a reputation for being a tough guy when he was just thirteen years old after he knocked a grown man out cold for calling mama a bitch. Even though our mother was not very good to us, Duck was a mama's boy. He would fight anyone when it came to mama or any of his sisters. He was very protective of us girls, especially me because he knew what I had gone through during our childhood. He made it a point to let all of his friends and the guys in our neighborhood know that his sisters were off limits.

He was also the breadwinner in our house. He kept our lights on, food in the refrigerator and clothes on our backs. We no longer had to worry about moving often because Duck made sure our rent was paid each month. Although he was young, he took good care of each of us so we respected him as the man of the house. Whatever profits he made in the streets was shared with us, like a father caring for his kids.

In some ways, I believe Duck turned to selling drugs as a means of survival. He and I often talked about how bad our life was and how much we wanted everything to change. He forbade any of us from following in his foot stops, which is why he did not want any of his sisters dating any of his associates.

After Charles approached me that day on the bus stop, we practically spent every day together. We could not get enough of each other. When we first started dating, Charles was different from any of the other boys in the neighborhood. Deep down he was very intelligent and caring, but he had to hide this about himself in order to survive in our neighborhood. There was nothing hip or cool about being smart. I could not believe he was interested in me, but he was.

We had a movie-like romance like the ones where the man sweeps the woman off her feet. He took good care of me and gladly let it be known to others that I was his girlfriend. Duck didn't like it too much at first but he knew I was happy so he let us be. After about six months of us dating, I learned I was pregnant with our first child. Shortly thereafter, he was arrested for dealing drugs and was sentenced to a year in jail.

A few days before he was to report to jail, we took the bus downtown to the Cook County courthouse and got married. We did not tell anyone about our plans, mainly because nobody else cared. Our mothers weren't in attendance because they both were too busy trying to score their next bag of drugs. We loved each other and were determined to be together and that was all that mattered to us.

After he reported to jail, I moved in with his mother because she lived closer to the county jail where he was serving his time. I visited him nearly every day and did my very best to write him letters. I could barely read or write but that did not matter to either of us.

His mother helped me a little during the pregnancy but I was mostly on my own. I even had to deliver our child, a boy I named after Charles, on my own. I stayed in labor for more than 10 hours without any pain medication because I did not have a medical card. Eventually the doctors decided to give me a cesarean section because my labor was not progressing and the baby was showing signs of distress.

I was all alone and scared for my life because I did not have any emotional support and I did not know what to expect. I was afraid that the pain would kill me. I did not know how my small frame would deliver a full-grown baby. I was nauseous and shaking while lying there in the bed hooked up to all of those scary machines. Luckily, I was heavily sedated and unaware of what was going on during the procedure.

When I awoke from the anesthesia a team of doctors stood hovering over me as if I was on exhibit at the DuSable Museum. They told me I almost died. Apparently, my body went into shock from the medicine. I was given too much anesthesia and my body rejected it. I made a full recovery but mentally that situation still haunts me to this day.

I had to learn how to be a mother on the fly, even after raising my sisters and brothers, my own child made me forget what it was like to care for a baby. I decided to drop out of school, which wasn't a hard decision for me because I didn't have much use for school. Besides, I barely went anyway. I got a job at a local car wash as a detailer. Charles' mother would babysit for me while I worked but she did not provide any other help. She made it clear that my baby was solely my responsibility. I paid rent and gave her all of the money and food stamps I received from public aid. My salary was just enough to buy diapers, wipes, formula and clothes for the baby.

By the time Charles Jr. was nearing his first birthday, Charles Sr. was released from jail. Sadly, the Charles that was released from Cook County jail was not the same man I had fallen in love with. The new Charles was easily angered, impatient, physically and emotionally abusive and distant. He was no longer caring and attentive to my needs. Instead, he seemed to take all of his frustrations and anger out on me. I could never do anything to his liking.

I did my best to overlook the way he was treating me because I knew something terrible happened to him while he was in jail. Based on my own experiences, I believed he had been sexually abused but was too ashamed to say anything or get help. He frequently had violent nightmares that caused him to awake in cold sweats.

He was also abusing drugs in order to cope. Prior to going to jail he refused to drink alcohol or use drugs. While all of his friends found it cool to smoke weed, he vehemently refused to partake. He hated drugs and alcohol because of how it destroyed his family. Now he could not start his day without smoking weed laced with cocaine and a beer.

He would stay away from home for days at a time. When he was home all he would do was eat, sleep all day, and run the streets at night. I could not ask where he had been, where he was going, or when he planned to return. My only job was to obey him by opening my legs whenever he told me to.

Chapter 7

Over the course of our 20 year marriage, we had four children; Charles Jr., Kenyatta, Jamal, and Lucas, all of whom I birthed and raised on my own. After all that I endured birthing Charles Jr., delivering the others, also via cesarean section, was a piece of cake. I had grown used to doing everything on my own. At night, while they slept, I cried and quietly vented my frustrations to God.

By the time Jamal was born I worked up the courage to move into my own apartment. The conditions at his mother's apartment were deplorable, infested with mice and roaches. She smoked crack out in the open for the kids to see and her bedroom door revolved just as often as my mother's had. I had also grown tired of handing over all of my public aid money to her and still having to pay her to babysit the kids whenever I needed to run an errand.

Charles did not work and refused to provide any financial assistance to me or our kids because he knew I received public aid. Over the years he became a serial cheater and often bounced between me and numerous other women. He even fathered multiple children outside of our marriage. He eventually became strung out on drugs often smoking more than he sold.

I grew so accustomed to his ways that the cheating did not bother me. At times I was relieved when he left me to be with other women because then I had peace. I was always anxious whenever he was home because he would beat me if the kids were being too loud or if he was frustrated about anything. I always had to hide any money I had because he would take it from me. There were times where he would take my public aid check and I had to struggle to pay rent.

We moved often because I developed a bad habit of my own. I was not pressured or forced into using drugs, I did them because I wanted to. I needed an outlet from the train-wreck that was my life. I often experienced flashbacks of all the abuse and mistreatment I suffered throughout my entire life. Using drugs allowed me to forget about everything and live freely without the painful memories of the past bringing me down. I was able to escape my insecurities and our troublesome marriage filled with lies, infidelity, and abuse. I was suffering from depression and PTSD, but did not know it.

One day Charles came home, packed up all of his belongings and walked out on us for good without saying a word or even leaving a note. The kids were in school and I was meeting with my new caseworker at the public aid office. We had just moved into an apartment in Gary, Indiana, which was a foreign place to me. I had never been outside of Chicago. We hadn't even finished unpacking everything. I realized he was gone for good when I noticed imprints in the carpet leading to our front door, which let me know he hauled his safe away. He kept his most prized possessions in that safe.

He always threatened to leave often staying away for several days at a time, but he always left the safe behind claiming it was too heavy to move. The safe served as my reassurance that he would return. Instantly my stomach sank and tears streamed uncontrollably down my face upon seeing the imprints in the carpet. I cried because I feared for my own and the children's well-being. Also, because I was somehow still in love with him and hoped everything would get better. The more he mistreated and cheated on me the harder I worked to please him. I called around to everyone connected to him but no one had heard from him or knew where he was.

My state of panic and out of control behavior in that moment reminded me of Uncle June's sorrow and helplessness when he learned about daddy's death. My emotions turned from sadness and depression to anger. The nerve of him to leave me with four kids after all that I had taken from him over the years. I did not know anyone who lived in Gary, Indiana and I did not know what to do.

We stayed there in Gary, Indiana until the property owner threatened to evict us and call children and family services on me. By then I allowed the drugs to take over my life. I turned into my mother, drinking, drugging and leaving my kids home alone for days at a time while I binged. I even became abusive toward them when I could not get money for drugs or if they made too much noise while I tried to sleep. I was a monster out of control. I could not stop myself from the destruction. I watched Charles Jr. turn into me when I was his age.

He had to grow up quickly because the others needed him. Unlike me, he did not have his dad to fall back on. Instead, he developed a relationship with Uncle June's wife, Joanne. Unbeknownst to me he communicated with her on a regular basis, informing her of everything that was going on in our household. By this time she and Uncle June had long been divorced but she still had a good relationship with the family. I could have passed out when I heard a knock at our door and she was standing on the other side looking at me with disdain in her eyes.

Charles Jr. told her about the eviction notice and the possibility of child services stepping in to take them away. She offered to take them while I take time to get myself together which meant getting off drugs. I put up very little resistance because I was relieved. Now I had the freedom to be out in the streets whenever I desired without having to feel guilty about leaving them alone. I did not have to hide my drugs or the fact that I was drunk or high. Most importantly I did not have to hide from Charles Jr.

He was a smart kid so I really was not hiding anything from him. He always knew the truth about why I could not sit still or why they had to be quiet all the time or why I disappeared for two or three days at a time. I no longer had to deal with the guilt of dodging the landlord because I spent the rent money on cocaine.

When Charles Sr. left I went into a downward spiral and could never quite pull myself out. Instead, I sank deeper and deeper and lost myself in the midst of it all. Even to this day I am trying to recover from the emotional wounds of the past. I've made it a habit to turn to drugs for comfort and release. The first high after Charles left was the best I ever had. I felt like I was sitting on the clouds watching the world move in slow motion beneath me. I spent the better part of the next 20 years chasing that same high but it would never come.

Along the way, I would visit with my kids from time to time. Chicago was known for its periods of bad weather. During those times when the weather was severe Joanne always felt sorry for me and allowed me to stay with the kids for a few weeks at a time. I slept all day and walked the streets at night looking to score. She complained to me in private, careful not to upset my children. By now they were growing older and more aware of what my drug habit was doing to my life. They were ashamed of what I had become. They still loved me but were careful not to let on to their friends or others, who knew nothing about me, that I was their mother - a junkie.

I could never be mad at them for being ashamed of me because they had every right. They did not deserve all of the unfortunate blows life had dealt them. One Saturday morning I decided to surprise my oldest son, Charles Jr, at the park where he played basketball every week. I put on my best clothes and fixed my hair as best I could. I stood off to the side of the small crowd watching as he dribbled the big, orange ball with ease while sticking his tongue out like his favorite player, Michael Jordan. I do not know much about basketball, or any other sport, but he seemed to be a step ahead of everyone else. He drained shot after shot without the ball hitting the rim. None of the other boys could seem to guard him. I was proud of him and could not believe he was part of me.

In that moment, I felt sick to my stomach, embarrassed, and ashamed of myself. I was also sad that I had not paid more attention to my kids and showed more interest in their interests. I chased after Charles Sr. throughout their childhood then moved on to drugs without consideration for them. In the process, they had all grown up and formed into people I did not know. Replaying all of my parenting mistakes in my head brought on tears. I cried right there in the park because I wanted to change but that sentiment made me crave drugs even more.

ROCK BOTTOM

As Charles Jr. and his friend approached the area where I was standing I decided to let him see me. Wiping away the tears from my face I prepared to embrace him. We met eyes for a brief second but he proceeded to walk passed me as if I were just another stranger passing by. He gave me a look of disdain as his eyes told me "stay away and don't say a word." He casually walked about talking with his friend and twirling the orange ball on one finger as if he did not have a care in the world. It was as if his mama was not a cracked out junkie and his father had not walked away from the family. My presence did not seem to affect him one way or another. My feet were like lead, I wanted to reach out and say something but I could not move. I stared until he and his friend disappeared past a couple holding hands, then the little kids dribbling the mini basketballs.

I felt distraught because then it was apparent that he did not want to have anything to do with me. I did what I always did in these types of situations. I went straight to my dealer and begged for drugs on credit. Drugs always soothed my pain and made the demons disappear. Soon after that encounter with Charles Jr., I decided to stay away from Joanne and the kids until I could get myself right. It felt good in knowing they were safe so I did not worry. I was free from her guilt trips and her worrying about my comings and goings. Selfishly, I wanted to live my life my way without having to consider anyone else.

Chapter 8

I was out living my life and going from pillar to post. The days turned into weeks, weeks into months, and months into years without a word from me. I missed birthdays, holidays, graduations, and even the birth of my first grandchild, Keisha. I did not meet her for the first time until she was more than a year old. I was absent, strung out on drugs and even signed away my parental rights to Joanne. My baby boy, Lucas was twelve years old; Joanne was the only mother he had ever known.

The older children, one-by-one, deserted me. They even went as far as referring to Joanne as mama and me by my first name. This hurt me tremendously but I understood it, I had not done my part as their mother. They wanted me to suffer in the same way I caused them to suffer. Joanne was doing the things I was supposed to be doing. She made sure they had a full stomach each night, shelter, clothing and love. She nursed them back to health whenever they were sick. I resented her for many years because my kids seemed to have more love for her; even though I was well aware of how she stepped up and took them in even after all of my blood relatives turned their backs on us.

Lucas always had serious problems with wetting the bed that seemed to get worse as he got older. Joanne became concerned when she noticed his urine was brown in color and carried a strong odor. She had him evaluated and he was diagnosed with stage 4 bladder cancer at the age of 13. The doctors gave him six months to live. She tracked me down to deliver the terrible news which sent me to my knees. I could not comprehend it so I refused to accept it. Instead, I did more drugs than usual to block out my fears that he would die.

I accompanied him to all of his treatments and cared for him when he became too weak to get out of bed. I spent my days answering to his every request and my nights sobbing quietly because of the heavy burden I carried knowing I failed my children. I was trying to make up for all of the wrong I caused, so none of his demands were off limits. I could not handle the grief that I was feeling in watching my child suffer and wither away before my very eyes. Each day he seemed to fade away to where I could no longer recognize him.

Then came those words, "If you ever want to see me alive again you better get up here now", he spoke weakly into the phone. Those words pierced through my soul as I dropped to my knees begging God not to take my baby away. I hung up the phone, smoked the last of what I had left in my crack pipe and headed for the county hospital. Along the way, I drank a pint of Hennessey straight out of the bottle to calm my nerves and keep me from crying.

My stomach sank as I entered the room and saw him lying there helpless, weak, and fading away. My other boys, and of course Joanne, were all there huddled around his bed waiting for the moment when he would quietly slip away. Joanne embraced me at the door with a bear hug. She held me tight as she knew the inevitable was upon us. I could tell she was emotional because for once she did not scold me for smelling of alcohol, and she did not search my eyes to see whether I was under the influence of drugs. The other boys kept quiet and talked amongst themselves making me feel like an unwanted visitor. I was too drunk and emotionally drained to care at that moment.

I slowly approached his bed contemplating whether I could handle the situation. One part of me felt strong enough while the other wanted to break down. I fought with myself mentally because I did not want him to see me lose it. My knees buckled along the way but I was able to stand tall and kept the tears from falling. Somehow, I felt a little better because when my eyes met his, without a word, he let me know that everything would be ok. He was at peace with his death.

In silence, I held his hand and watched as his chest went up and down while he slept. During the short periods he was awake he was too weak to talk. As I watched over him I recalled all of the good memories. Although there were few I purposed in my heart to cherish them. I fantasized about how I could be a better mother to him and the others.

I was desperate in my heart thinking that if I could miraculously come up with a cure for cancer I would have Lucas healed right then. Within that hour of my arrival at the hospital he took his last breath. I'll never forget the blaring sound of the breathing machine beeping indicating that Lucas was no longer breathing.

The medical staff rushed into the room knowing there was no hope for resuscitation. He was pronounced dead at 10:19pm that night, which was eerie because that was the exact same time he was born. I dropped to my knees and screamed out in agony as everyone else sobbed loudly mourning the loss of our baby. I remember when I found out that Lucas was sick that I bargained with God to take me instead of him, but God had other plans. Selfishly, I did everything to sabotage my life so that I would not have to deal with the agony of seeing my son die.

The doctors allowed us to stay with his body for a short while to say our good-byes. My legs went numb and all that I ate or drank came up. I begged and pleaded with the doctors to allow me to go with him as they tried to wheel his lifeless body down the long hallway. For years, I would relive this moment repeatedly in my mind. I have not had a decent night's sleep since, wondering how alone he must have felt in his final moments. Even with a room full of people present knowing he would leave this world alone.

For the next five years I lived on the edge of darkness with a death wish. I spent every day either drunk or high because I could not deal with the fact that I left my kids, my son died alone, and I was a junkie. I even resorted to stealing from stores and running credit card swindles for money to buy drugs. I was willing to do anything to keep my habit going. I believed I deserved to die instead of Lucas. I was no good for my kids or society, so I intentionally put myself in dangerous situations hoping to die.

Once Lucas died my contact with my children came to a halt. I knew that Joanne would take good care of them so I thought it best that I stay away. I was living from on the streets anyway and believed that I did not have anything to offer them. I even lived in abandoned buildings when I did not have anywhere to go. I also chose not to pursue relationships with men. Men seemed to be my downfall so I tried by best to avoid them dealing with them.

I desperately wanted to get clean so that I could return to my children in a way they could accept. However, my addiction had a strong hold on me and I could not break free.

One day I decided to pick up and move to another part of the city, close to where my siblings and I lived when we stayed with Uncle Maurice and his family. I figured a fresh start in a new area would put me on the road to sobriety. I kept in touch with a few friends from my old neighborhood but I was careful to distance myself.

Unbeknownst to me I was setting myself up to enter into a new journey that would land me right back where I started - penniless and at rock bottom.

Chapter 9

Kevin was short, bald-headed, and handsome – he was charming without saying a word and that's what got me. I noticed him right away as I approached Kurt's corner store early one Saturday morning. I had never seen Kevin around the neighborhood before. He was standing there talking to Mr. McGee, a friendly older man who was known to love the young women in the neighborhood. He was also known to talk your ear off, too.

I was going to buy a few items for Mr. Calhoun, an old man I had befriended and was caring for over the past two years. I was not looking my best; I was still wearing my headscarf, pajamas, and raggedy shoes. Trying not to be noticed, I swiftly made my way to the door after quickly saying hello to McGee praying he would not try to lure me into a long conversation. McGee loved to reminisce about the good ole days, especially his life after returning home from the Vietnam War. He lived in this area his entire life. He knew everything about everybody because he loved to gossip.

By the time I made it out of the store the handsome man was standing there by himself leaning against a car watching the entrance to Kurt's store. He looked as if he was waiting for me to come out.

"Hey, you need some help carrying those bags, mama?" He asked.

I quickly shot back, "No, I got it." Giving him a little attitude but secretly hoping he would persist. He had my attention but I could not let him know it.

"I don't know, mama. You being such a little lady I think you need my help." He said grabbing two bags out of my hand before I could respond.

His hand was soft and gentle. He looked at me as if he was seeing his first love for the first time. He had a calming nature about him that made me feel at ease. He put me in the mind of my daddy. He was wearing a white, button-up shirt; heavily creased, dark, denim Levi jeans; and black-suede buck shoes. His mustache was neatly trimmed and I could see my reflection off his baldhead. He looked and smelled good. I do not think he noticed but I was nervous, my palms were shaky and sweaty. My heart was beating so fast I thought it would jump out of my chest. As we walked in silence for a few moments my mind could not stop racing. I kept reminding myself that men never meant me any good, but something about him made me want to give up on my celibacy experiment that I had been doing for quite a while.

I had no idea what to say to this man. I lacked good self-esteem for as long as I could remember. I never saw myself as a good-looking woman. I had tumors spread over my entire body that looked like large bumps. I inherited Agent Orange, a form of skin cancer from my father; he was infected while serving in the Vietnam War. In addition, I was very skinny with a flat behind and smaller breast than other twelve-year-old girls. I remember being teased profusely growing up. My best asset was my long, pretty, curly hair. My mother would always tell me, "Debbie, God blessed you with good hair because you got a face only a mother could love. I'm your mother and I don't love it all that much." She would say with a sinister giggle. She always said shit like that to all six of us. She purposely wanted to break us down emotionally, especially me for some reason. She reminded me as often as she could that I was her worst looking girl. I knew I was not going to win anybody's beauty pageant but I was far from ugly in my own eyes.

"So when can I take you out? They play good music down there at Butler's Lounge. Can you dance, mama?" He asked, dancing a jig and flashing a Kool-Aid smile.

Snapping out of my trance I coldly responded, "I ain't yo' damn mama, so stop calling me that. Do I look like an old woman to you?"

Thinking about my mama always changed my mood for the worse. Even on my best days, which were few and far in between, thoughts of her could ruin my happiness. I had nothing but bad memories of her. I was still battling demons from my childhood caused by her. Even still it was my nature to be feisty, especially toward men. I refused to allow myself to come off as weak or a pushover; the streets taught me more about survival than anything else in my life. This man made me nervous because my body started to feel all of the same feelings I felt when I first met Charles.

"Oh, I like 'em feisty! You and me gon' get along just fine." He said through that same Kool-Aid smile of his. He smiled practically the whole time we had been talking. This made it harder and harder for me to keep my stoic demeanor. I was actually enjoying his company. His smile was so wide I could see he desperately needed dental work more so than I did. I had been hit in the mouth so many times by Charles Sr. that I was missing two of my bottom teeth, which was causing the others to bunch up in the middle. My mouth did not look too bad but I did not do a whole lot of smiling.

"I ain't never seen you around here before." I said looking him up and down with a scowl on my face searching his body as if I could discover a secret he was trying to keep from me. I wanted to be tough in order to send the message that I could not be fucked with.

"Forgive me, sweetheart. My name is Kevin Scott Bradley. I grew up around here over on Emerald Street. Matter of fact my brother, Gary, works for Kurt and you just saw me talking to McGee. You know don't nothing get past ole McGee." He said confidently. Then he started naming people from the neighborhood until it became clear to me that he was very familiar with the area. By this time we reached the old man's apartment above Butler's Lounge. I thanked him for helping me, grabbed my bags and disappeared up the stairs.

"So can I take you out or what? What's your number?" He called after me. "I know you ain't gone leave me hanging out here, mama," He said desperately. "I promise I am a nice guy. Ask around, the neighborhood will tell you. I just want to get to know you that's all. Can I at least use your bathroom? I don't think it would be very gentlemanly of me to pee in the alley!" He yelled standing there waiting for me to return.

I kept walking as if I did not hear a word. He stood there a few moments longer before walking off toward Emerald Street looking defeated.

I watched until he disappeared pass the trees. Part of me wanted to call after him and continue to allow him the chance to court me. I was interested in him but I would not allow myself to act on it because I did not think he was into my lifestyle. At that time I was still abusing crack cocaine and I was too ashamed to allow him to know. I primarily hung out with other addicts but I did not want to be with anybody who was just as strung out as I was. I was never romantically interested in any of the men I routinely got high with anyway. My outlook on men had always been a poor one. I did not trust them as far as I could see them.

Chapter 10

I was living with and taking care of Mr. Calhoun, but we were not lovers contrary to popular belief. People in the neighborhood often whispered about sexual services they thought I was supplying to Calhoun. Our relationship was never of a sexual nature. He was more like a father figure to me. Nothing about cleaning that old man's ass was appealing to me. Besides, he had not even been out of the bed for more than a few minutes at a time in the two years I had been caring for him.

Mr. Calhoun owned an A&P Deli located on the corner of 119th & Emerald Street on the Southside of the city. This was not the same A&P Deli that Duck and I dug in the garbage can when we were kids. Mr. Calhoun gave me a job as a cashier when I relocated to the area after leaving my kids. He was a kind and gentle man always willing to help someone in need, especially if he thought you were trying to do something positive with your life. He treated me like a human being and never tried anything sexual, which was foreign to me. Outside of my daddy, nearly every man I have been in contact with since I was 10 years old tried me sexually, except him. For that reason alone I always respected the old man.

Mr. Calhoun was a devoted family man who honored his late wife, Mildred and their children. He always had a cool, calm demeanor and never spoke badly about anyone. He employed many young people from the neighborhood but some took his kindness for weakness. Several of his workers stole money from the cash register and gave away free food to their friends and family. Even in those situations he never raised his voice or lost his temper. Instead, he would say a special prayer to the "good Lord" and keep moving forward. He was a very spiritual man who attended church every Sunday and prayed daily. The old man had so much faith in God that I became a stronger believer. As a child I remember praying a lot, but faith never followed. I believe my lack of faith was because of my circumstances - they never changed for the better no matter how hard I prayed. I felt as if my prayers were going unanswered. But Mr. Calhoun somehow was able to put a small light back into my faith and trust in God for a while.

When I found out Mr. Calhoun was sick and needed a caregiver I did not hesitate to rush to his side. I practically worked for free. He provided food and shelter but I never asked him for money. I did not have to because he made sure that I had everything I needed. I felt like I owed it to him to give him my acts of service because he had always been so good to me. Besides, I enjoyed caring for others, especially elderly people like Mr. Calhoun. He worked hard his entire life, but his now failing health would not allow him to live independently any longer.

He never bothered me for anything unless he absolutely needed my help. For the first few months of me moving in with him he was still able to get around the house and care for himself to some extent. He was just afraid of being alone because he had fallen a few times before and could not get to the phone right away. Then after his heart weakened he became totally bed ridden. He could only get out of bed to use the bathroom but often times he would not make it there in time. As a result he was forced to wear diapers, which hurt him tremendously. For the first few months, he would cry during every changing because he did not feel it was appropriate for me to see his genitals. He looked at me as if I were one of his daughters or a niece. He also had trouble accepting his loss of independence and having to rely on someone else to care for him.

Taking care of him turned out to be one of the best decisions of my life. I am certain that moving in with him saved my life. I had been taking chances sleeping in abandoned buildings. I have never had any family members that I could turn to in my times of need. Rather than running to any of them and getting my feelings hurt, I took my chances and hoped the Lord would watch over me. In a weird sort of way, I enjoyed the freedom of not having to pay bills and still being able to live independently. I liked not having to answer to anyone. Living on the streets as a woman was still tough, though. I often had to move from one building to another whenever I felt I was in danger. Every now and then the media would flood the area to report on stories about women being raped and sometimes killed in the area, but I made sure to keep a low profile and paid close attention to my surroundings.

To protect myself I changed my location often. In the wee hours of the morning I would move my suitcases and other possessions a little at a time to a new location. I was very careful about keeping my living quarters a secret because I did not trust too many people. Amazingly, nobody ever bothered me and none of my belongings ever disappeared. I did not have a bed so I made a comfortable pallet out of old mats a daycare center sat in the alley for trash. I kept a few dishes, blankets, sheets and small decorations from my apartment. Wherever I decided to settle I did my best to make it feel like a home.

I hung pictures of my kids on the wall, put up small decorations around the holiday, and I used a cooler to keep my food cold. I stole my tissue, dishwashing liquid, cleaning supplies and other toilettes from big department stores on the other side of town. I was well known throughout my neighborhood so it would not have been wise of me to steal from stores in my area. I would ride the EL train two to three times a week to beg for money. Sometimes I would get enough money to buy what I needed outright including drugs. I like to think of myself as an honest person but I did what I had to do.

Every now and then I would luck up on an abandoned building where the water was still on. I stayed at these places the longest. There I could hand wash my clothes and take a decent bath. Otherwise, I would steal water from nearby houses during early morning hours. Even though I was homeless I tried to keep myself clean.

Like old times, I put an empty box in the window facing the alley to distinguish my building from the others. In a weird sort of way, this provided me warmth and comfort because it reminded me of home. Even though it was a dysfunctional home, it was still home.

The winter months were the worst, not only because of the cold weather, but because of rodents. Some of the rats were just as big as small cats. I constantly had to run stray cats and dogs out of my place. They were able to get in through broken windows and raggedy doors. I managed to make the best of my situation, which was a blessing in disguise because it taught me to be strong. I was being prepared for the tough road ahead.

Chapter 11

I would see Kevin around the neighborhood from time to time. We would exchange a few words but nothing major. He was always neat, clean, and well groomed. He seemed to be a good catch but I dared not to pursue him romantically for fear he would find out about my habit. After all the dodging I was doing in trying not to let him find out about me, I was surprise to see him one night in the same area where I buy my drugs. Only known drug users frequented the area, which let me know he also used drugs.

Once the cat was out of the bag for both of us we started hanging out on a regular basis getting high together. We did not become a couple right away, he was more like a good male friend. He would walk with me back and forth to the store, make small repairs around the apartment, and even permed my hair a few times for me. He was a true jack-of-all-trades.

One Saturday night we got so high I passed out. I woke up butt naked with him on top of me thrusting inside of me like there was no tomorrow. I didn't remember taking off my clothes or agreeing to have sex with him. He did not seem to be bothered that I wasn't participating. I laid there searching my mind trying to figure out what was going on. I did not know whether to scream, cry, or moan because it felt good, or get up and run and never look back. I did not understand what was going on. I knew I liked him but I wasn't ready to go as far as sex.

Suddenly I heard a loud groan and he collapsed beside me. I figured it was over. I could not get back to sleep so I laid there crying silent tears, debating whether I should continue seeing him or report him to the police for rape. How could it be rape if my body enjoyed it in a weird sort of way? I actually liked him and would have eventually had sex with him. However, I was upset that he did not give me the opportunity to decide whether I wanted to be intimate with him. Then I convinced myself I was a willing participant.

Ultimately, I tucked it away in my memory bank and moved on.

He never spoke a word about what happened that night. I wondered sometimes what if he was so high he did not remember either. Without any discussion we became a couple. In the beginning our relationship was beautiful. He was very kind, gentle, and loving. He was my protector. We were like any other couple, we went out to eat, to the drive-in movies – we just could not get enough of each other. We even had pet names for each other and kissed so often people thought we were Siamese twins. You did not see him without me.

I met his kids and ex-wife, Brenda, early into the relationship. She wasn't the mad woman he painted her out to be. In fact, she seemed to show genuine concern for me whenever we would visit her and the kids. I found it odd that she referred to him as Dr. Jekyll and Mr. Hyde. She always looked me up and down as if she was searching my body for bruises or something. She would even ask questions like, "Is the honeymoon still going on? Have you been introduced to the real Kevin? Does he allow you to leave the house alone, yet?" Then she gave me advice, "Don't let him dictate everything. Let him know that you're strong. Always stand your ground with him." I had no idea what she was talking about but she did put something on my mind. Of course, one day I would come to understand why she was asking me all of those questions.

I started to notice he always had to be in control of everything. I couldn't go anywhere alone. He would ask for a detailed run down of my conversations with anyone I talked to. He always wanted me near him. He told me several times that he wanted me all to himself. In the beginning I thought this was cute. I mistook it for love because no one had ever showed that much interest in me. I couldn't get enough of him and he was the same with me. I didn't realize that I had become so engrained in his world that I no longer had an identity of my own.

I was so caught up in him that I even stopped hanging out with my best girlfriend, Sharon. We had been friends since childhood. We did everything together before I met Kevin. Sharon, like me, had a rough upbringing and was addicted to crack cocaine as well. We were more like sisters than friends. She was the godmother to all of my children just as I was to hers. We depended on one another for love and support because we were very distant from our families.

Kevin never admitted he did not want Sharon around but I knew he didn't. Whenever I would mention her name or she would call me on the phone or stop by the apartment it seemed like he would get an attitude. He would go from very talkative to quiet and standoffish when Sharon was around. We could be cuddling on the couch enjoying each other's company, but if the phone rang and it was Sharon his whole mood changed in an instant. To please him I started avoiding Sharon and ignoring her phone calls. I was hoping things would change once the newness of our relationship wore off. Instead his controlling nature only got worse.

Sharon must have caught on because she stopped coming over to visit and her calls became less and less. I was surprised when she invited us to her birthday party. I knew he wouldn't want to go so I planned to go alone. I caught him in a good mood one day. I told him I wanted to go by Sharon's party that Saturday night for a little while. I don't know why, but I was nervous to ask. My palms were sweaty just as they had been the day I met him and I felt like I had to get his permission. He didn't say much at first, he just got quiet before finally muttering "okay" with a shrug of his shoulders. I felt very relieved. I was happy he didn't object because I missed Sharon.

On the day of the party he was not acting like himself. He complained about the breakfast I made that morning. Suddenly the TV was up too loud and I was spending too much time in the room with Calhoun. He was nitpicking about everything. Then he started accusing me of cheating with different men in the neighborhood. I laughed it off saying, "you're crazy," as I stood at the kitchen sink washing dishes. The next thing I knew I was on the ground gasping for air trying to break free of his hands wrapped tightly around my neck.

"Bitch, you think that shit is funny? Who is laughing now, huh? Who is laughing now, huh? You dirty motherfucker you. I should knock your ass out." He said looking into my eyes as I lay there on the floor dazed and confused. He had me pinned underneath him. I stared in his eyes begging and pleading for my life. There was nothing there. It was as if he was an entirely different person. When my eyes started rolling to the back of my head he let me go. He got up and walked out the door as if nothing happened. Now I knew first-hand what Brenda had been alluding to all along.

This was the first time he had ever hit me. For some reason I wasn't surprised by his actions. In fact, I knew it was coming but I did not think it would be that bad. I did not think he would ever try to kill me. He had called me a bitch a few times, but always apologized profusely afterwards.

I had no clue of what to do. At this point I needed Sharon the most but I didn't want to ruin her birthday party. Besides, I felt bad about avoiding her all that time. I was too emotional to go to the party and my eyes were puffy from crying so much. I also noticed several scratches on my neck. I spent the whole night getting high by myself. I needed to take my mind away from all of the confusion. I contemplated putting all of his stuff in the hallway and never letting him back in. I was not surprised when he did not come back to the apartment that night. I hoped he would stay away.

The next morning I went out to get the Sunday paper and there he was sleep in the hallway smelling like a liquor store. He looked very peaceful, almost tranquil laying there on the dirty floor. My heart melted all over again the way it did when I first laid eyes on him. Somehow, I started doubting myself, thinking maybe I drove him to hit me. Before he opened his eyes I made it up in my mind that I would take him back. I reasoned with myself, the man loves you, Debbie. Everybody makes mistakes. I had been through much worse with Charles and he didn't care half as much about me as Kevin does - I reminded myself. Shedding tears he promised to, "Never lay another hand on me. I will always honor you as my woman, mama. You mean everything to me." He professed to me and I believed him.

Everything went back to normal except he was getting high more often. Then after a few weeks he started going out without me. I knew better than to question him but I could feel that things in our relationship were starting to change. He was the type of man who didn't believe in answering to his woman. He ruled with an iron fist. Even though he was going out more often he expected me to sit at home and watch TV all day, every day.

Sharon eventually confronted me about missing her birthday party. He was in the next room so I could not talk to her the way I really wanted. She was pressing me about missing her party declaring he was controlling my life. He had to have been listening to our conversation because out of nowhere he snatched the phone from my ear and told her, "Bitch, don't call here no more. Debbie got a man now, she don't have to explain shit to you." Then he hung up the phone and told me, "Don't you even dream of calling that

bitch back. You don't need friends. I am all that you need."
He had the same look of rage in his eyes as the night he choked me out.

Once again, I knew not to question or go against him. I did as I was told and stayed away from Sharon. If I saw her on the street, I went a different route. If she called on the telephone, I let it ring until the voicemail message came on. Each time she tried to contact me I died a little inside, she was my best friend, the only person I had to lean on in tough times. Yet I continued to push her away to please him. I did whatever he wanted but I repeatedly fell short in his eyes. He often put others that I did not approve of ahead of me without regard for my feelings.

Gradually his moods started to change putting me on edge. One moment he could be the sweetest most caring and loving man in the world that would do anything for me. Then the moment something did not go his way he would become a very different person. I could be "the dumbest bitch in the world" one day and "baby, mama, or boocka" the next. I never knew what his mood would be. Sometimes everything could change in an instant without warning. He was like a ticking time bomb that could explode at any time. I was always anxious, but I learned to adapt just as I had to do growing up.

Mr. Calhoun died from a heart attack three days after Christmas. I found his lifeless body slumped over in his bed with a Bible in his hand. He had a peaceful look on his face. He was a very spiritual man who prayed for everybody. He took me in and treated me like a daughter. Until I met Kevin, I always put his needs first even when I wanted to get high or if I was coming down off of a high. I would somehow muster up the energy to do whatever he requested. He was a genuinely good person who treated everyone with respect no matter one's lifestyle.

When Kevin moved in everything about my relationship with Calhoun changed. Mr. Calhoun was very old and feeble. He depended on me to care for him. However, I could not allow him to be my main priority because I had to focus on keeping Kevin happy. Kevin declared, "that old man can do more for himself but he chooses not to because he knows you're going to do everything for him." All of the personal care tasks that he relied on me to do he was left to do them on his own.

I wore myself out trying to cater to both of them, but I often fell short. There were days when Mr. Calhoun didn't get his heart medication and baths were few and far in-between. He felt powerless and I did not stand up for him. I believe that is what ultimately led to his death.

Kevin seemed to go out of his way to make the old man miserable. He liked to raise his voice and argue with me every chance he got, even after I explained to him that Calhoun did not like loud noise because it reminded him of his time fighting in World War II. A few weeks before his death, Calhoun gave me an ultimatum that either Kevin had to leave or he was going to move into a nursing home.

Chapter 12

Our apartment became the hang out spot. Every Friday night Kevin hosted a card game for his friends and family. Loud music, cursing, drinking, smoking and shit talking were all a constant. A fight usually broke out and the police had to be called out several times. We got more attention from law enforcement than the dope house that was in the building next to ours. I had to be the host, meaning I did not get to rest until the last person was gone, which could be anywhere from 5am to 7am the next morning.

Calhoun practically had to fend for himself on weekends. When we weren't partying and playing cards we were getting high. I did a good job of hiding my addiction from him before Kevin and I started dating, but after the beatings started it became obvious. In the past I would not do my drugs in the apartment. Out of respect for the old man I would either go to the dope house or Sharon's. After my relationship became tumultuous I started to do my thing wherever I wanted in the apartment, except in Calhoun's bedroom.

Even though he was a sickly man he still had his full mind. He knew exactly what was going on in his place. He just could not do anything about it. He did not have any family or close friends to look after him. All of his kids lived out of state and did not seem to be interested in caring for him. He was at my mercy because I was all that he had. Therefore, he had no choice but to put up with our bullshit. I understand it all would have been different if his kids were more interested in his well-being. He did not deserve to live out his last days the way he did. I am still haunted by the way I allowed him to be treated, especially since he had been so good to me.

I believe he was afraid of Kevin, too. Kevin never said too much to Calhoun but he let it be known that he was in charge. He paid close attention to Calhoun's health and often asked questions about his family. Kevin was very observant to notice the old man never had any visitors other than his doctors and nurses. Before long, he moved into the apartment without asking permission. He came to spend a weekend and never left. The next thing I knew he moved all of his stuff in without an explanation or discussion. He even wrote his name on the mailbox.

Soon after he moved in he allowed his brothers, sisters, and other various family members to come and stay from time to time. Every other week we had a new person living with us wearing out the expensive leather furniture. The furniture became run down to the point where the leather was starting to tear. He would say, "Baby, Dionte, Gary, Larry, Diane or Dominique is going to stay with us for a little while." I could not go against him so I would always nod my head in agreement without saying a word. None of them ever paid rent or contributed to the household.

Calhoun made a nice living working for the railroad retirement board and he still owned the A & P Deli on the Southside. His apartment was decorated very nicely. He had expensive suits, tailor-made clothes, leather coats, gator shoes, watches and other jewelry, fedora hats of nearly every color and all sorts of other nice things. He also had several rare baseball cards that were worth money. He had lots of money in the bank from his pension checks from the railroad, profits from his store, and the insurance money he received after his wife died seven years ago.

After all of Kevin's kinfolks started moving in Calhoun's valuables started disappearing. He was a short heavyset man, so for the life of me I could not figure out who they were selling his clothes to. Then I started seeing different people in the neighborhood wearing his jewelry and coats. I believe Kevin was in on some of the stealing. Every time something came up missing I would mention it to him, but he never had much to say. Since nobody ever went into his bedroom I started locking up his valuables in the closet.

I never allowed my addiction to drive me to the point of stealing anything from Calhoun. I did not have to steal because he treated me very well. If I did not have money to smoke I did not smoke, or I would go out and hustle by washing cars, babysitting, cleaning houses, running errands, whatever I had to do to get money. I was known throughout the neighborhood for doing odd jobs for the elderly, so I never had any difficulty with making a few dollars. I had always been able to support my own habit without resorting to taking from others.

When he died his kids came and got what was left of his stuff. They were just as evil and corrupt as the dope fiends that were stealing from him. He left me $10,000.00 in his will, which I had to go to court to get because his kids refused to let me have it. They could not believe he would leave me that amount of money even though I took care of him for over two years. I was there cleaning, wiping, and going back and forth to the doctor with him when they would not even call to see how he was doing. They only called when they needed something.

As soon as that check arrived in the mail Kevin took it from me as if it belonged to him. I didn't have any say about how the money would be spent. He got us an apartment because we had been staying with his mother since Calhoun died. She made it clear the day we arrived that she didn't want us there. I didn't want to be there anyway. She was strict and kept a kennel full of dogs. I got tired of being pent up in the room all day. The only positive about living there was he couldn't beat on me. His mother wouldn't allow that.

By that time I had become his punching bag whenever something didn't go right or if I talked back or got out of line. After each beating he would apologize and promise not to hit me again. Sometimes, he would go weeks at a time without so much as raising his voice to me. I knew the longer he went without hitting me the worse the next beating would be.

Our first night in our new apartment we got high and had sex all night off and on. We had a good time just the two of us. In the middle of the night I awoke to him screaming, "Bitch, get yo' ass up right now" as he threw punches at me. I could feel my mouth filling up with blood. My bottom lip swelled up so big it was damn near touching my nose. I was half asleep so I felt like it must've been a dream.

"Open your eyes, bitch, before I kill your motherfucking ass!" He screamed as he lifted my body from the mattress and slung me across the room like I was a rag doll.

Before I could gather myself he had his arms around my neck choking me saying, "Bitch, I should kill you right now." Through gasps for air I apologized profusely but I didn't know what I did wrong. My heart was beating so fast I thought it would explode. I could feel myself losing consciousness. He had that faraway look in his eyes again as if he was not there. Suddenly he snapped out of it and let me go. Lifting his 280-pound body off me in a low voice he said, "You're lucky", before he disappeared into the night.

As I had so many times before I laid there cursing him, crying for my daddy, and praying for God to take me away. My life had been so filled with pain that I couldn't take anymore. By then I heard a few of my children had left Chicago to be with their dad who was in poor health and living in Minnesota. I did not have a relationship with any of my siblings. Calhoun was gone and now I feared for my life.

I gathered myself and decided enough was enough. I wanted to be done with Kevin but first I had to figure out how to get my money from him. My plan was to run off to California and start my life over. I needed to get away from everything and everyone. I wanted desperately to clean up what was left of my life. I knew I couldn't do that in Chicago. Temptation lurked on every corner.

I always dreamt of palm trees and the California sunshine as a kid. I quickly realized this was nothing but a pipe dream. I barely knew how to write my own name and I could not read. I dropped out of school in tenth grade. I got tired of embarrassing myself and being teased. The other kids picked on me for being a slow learner and I do not think I ever got over that.

I went to search through his belongs hoping he would have left at least some of the money. My stomach dropped when I realized all of his stuff was gone. He had taken everything as if he didn't plan on coming back. For days I waited for him to return but he never showed up. He left me with no money to pay the rent and no explanation as to why the relationship was over. I should have been the one to leave. He was mistreating me. I was hurt all over again because I had given him all of me and he walked out without a word. This was deja-vu all over again.

I searched his different hang out spots around the neighborhood but I could not find him anywhere. My mind vacillated from being angry to concerned, to remorseful believing it was all my fault somehow, to heartbroken. I was having a war within myself and I did not know how to handle it all. I did not think I wanted to be with him anymore but after sometime I started to miss him.

My mind forgot about all of the beatings, verbal abuse and cheating. Instead, it kept reminding me of all the good things about him. I convinced myself he was a good person who had a hard time managing his anger. He would rub my feet, hold me tight at night, and shared his money and drugs with me. He was proud to let everyone know I was his woman. He insisted on holding my hand whenever we went out in public together. The man even washed my hair from time to time.

He had a special way of catering to me. When I met Kevin he changed my whole life. He taught me how to dress as a woman. He made sure I kept my appearance up. He took me out to restaurants like Applebee's, Chili's, and Red Lobster, and we always bought the latest movies from the bootleg man. To the average person these are all simple things but to me it was special. I had never experienced any of this before I met Kevin. He was a good man to me. He was also the cleanest drug addict I had ever known.

After being separated from Kevin for the time I found myself so caught up into drugs that I let myself go. I didn't wear the best of clothes and I wore my shoes until the soles wore off. I didn't care about my appearance because I did not desire a man. My sole focus was getting high. I even spent all of my money on drugs instead of buying food. I began to reminisce on how Kevin taught me how to enjoy life in spite of my addiction.

I had made up my mind and decided I wanted him back. I honestly believed I could get him to change his abusive ways. I was going to stick by my man no matter what. I fantasized about us getting married and moving to California together. I would have had this man's baby if he wanted me to even though I was too old to even consider having another baby. I had to let him know that I was willing to forgive him for the beating. I was going to do whatever he wanted me to do sexually so he wouldn't have to stray. I had to find him so that I could declare my love.

I became so desperate I decided to visit his oldest daughter, Danielle. He was closest to her of all his kids. I knew she would definitely be able to tell me where he was. Danielle is a smart, young woman who is wise beyond her years. Her daddy always spoke highly of her. Although he never said it to me, I knew she was his favorite. She was the go to person of her siblings, like a second mother to all of them. She helped to raise them because Kevin and their mother were both so strung out on drugs. Derrick, the youngest of their children, still calls Danielle mom.

I developed a special bond with Danielle. I related better with her than I did with most adults my own age. She loved her daddy but that didn't get in the way of the truth. She knew he was abusive toward me. He had been the same way with her mother. She would say to me, "Debbie, I don't know why you love my daddy so much. He's not a bad person but he will never be good to you. He has major issues with women."

Danielle greeted me with a hug and a quick peck on the cheek when I showed up to her studio apartment on the Northside of the city. However, she was not her usual cheerful self. She appeared to be troubled, almost as if she was in mourning. Watching her facial expressions I got a sick feeling in the pit of my stomach. I thought she was going to tell me something terrible had happened to her dad. Over the past year and a half he had been having really bad chest pains.

A few times after we got high he had to be rushed to the emergency room. On one of the last visits the doctor warned if he didn't stop using drugs he could die from a heart attack. The drugs were taking its toll on his heart. Thinking about this sent me into frenzy. I figured this had to be the reason why she was acting so remorseful. Before I knew it tears were streaming down my face, I could not control myself. I fell to my knees and cried like a baby. Danielle put her arms around me and held me like I was a baby.

This was not easy for Danielle because she was overweight. Over the past few months, she had been having problems with her knees. She couldn't fully bend them, so for her to bend down with me on the ground I knew she cared for me. She kept saying, through tears, "It's going to be ok. It is going to be ok. I am so sorry, Debbie." I thought I would lose control of my bladder I became so emotional. Danielle rarely cried so I knew it had to be true Kevin must have died.

I pleaded with God, "Please, Lord, don't let it be true. Oh, Lord please bring him back, Lord. Why him, Lord? Why did you take away my only true love?"

Through my tears, I could see a puzzled look on Danielle's face. She seemed to be surprised and amused by my emotional rant. Her mood went from concern to excitement as she tried to snap me out of my trance. She grabbed me by both arms and loudly proclaimed with a smile on her face "Debbie, my daddy ain't dead. Where did you hear that?" She asked. "I just got off the phone with him," she said.

My mood instantly turned from anguish to glee. I could not be happier. She did not share in my sentiment. Instead, she stared at me with a look of pity on her face. This made me wonder why she seemed so depressed when I walked in. I suddenly got a sick feeling in the pit of my stomach because I knew something was wrong. In a quiet tone I asked her, "Where is your daddy?" I was afraid to hear the answer to that question because women's intuition told me I would not like it.

She blurted out, "He is living with Pam. I thought you knew?" She said in a low tone of voice. Pam was some woman that he had met at a super bowl party a few months back. I had suspected him of cheating with her but I could never prove it at the time. He would disappear for hours at a time during the night. When I would question him about his whereabouts he would get mad. I knew not to press him too much because he would become violent. I suffered a couple of busted lips and black eyes for questioning him about Pam. He would say, "Stop asking me about that bitch." However, he never actually denied having a relationship with her.

He would leave the room to talk on the phone and he never left his phone unattended. Now it all made perfect sense, he was leading a double life.

Before I could fully process everything that Danielle was trying to tell me I grabbed my coat and ran out of the door. Hot with anger I ran a block and a half to the train station so I could go back to the Southside. I decided to confront them face to face. I knew exactly where she lived because I followed him there one night. When he ranged her bell I saw her peek out her window to see who it was. I wasn't surprised as I knew it had to be a woman he was sneaking out to see at 2am. At the time I didn't have the courage to confront Kevin about it.

Once on the train, I struggled to control my emotions. I was nervous, angry, and sad all at the same time. I even sobbed aloud a few times wondering how he could do me this way. I would sit for a few minutes and pace the rail car for a few minutes. I was an emotional wreck and it showed judging by the curious looks the other passengers were giving me.

I was so frantic I began to talk to myself, saying things like, "How could this motherfucker treat me this way." I even declared, "I hate him!" I also thought he had some nerve to just up and leave me after all I did for him and his family. He was even bold enough to take the money Calhoun left for me.

The more I talked to myself the angrier I became. My thoughts became violent as I convinced myself he no longer deserved to live. I figured I would be doing the entire world a favor if I ended his life. I wanted to inflict on him all of the pain and abuse he put me through during our relationship. I even thought about Mr. Calhoun because I always believed the stress of having Kevin and his family around lead to the old man's death.

After what felt like an eternity the redline train came to a screeching halt at the 95th Street terminal. I ran to get on the 119th Street bus, which would take me to my destination. By then my nerves began to settle down and my anger was replaced with anxiety. I had become so nervous my hands and legs were shaking uncontrollably. My stomach was also a mess. I felt as though I would vomit. Suddenly the idea of killing him seemed to be too drastic.

When the bus finally made it to my stop I had to convince myself to get off. I was losing my momentum and started to talk myself out of confronting them. Instead of going to Sharon's apartment I decided it was best to go home. I started toward my apartment with a pep talk going on in my head. I told myself, "You don't need him, Debbie. He'll be back begging you before the year is out. Get yourself together and move on." Finally I reached my apartment and began to turn my key in the front door when a voice told me not to punk out as I usually did in situations like this. I never stood up for myself.

Within a blink of an eye, I found myself standing at the back door of Pam's apartment. I don't know how I got there so fast, but somehow I made it to her apartment. I could hear their muffled voices inside. The door was unlocked so I allowed myself in when I realized they were in another part of the apartment. From the kitchen I followed their voices to the master bedroom where the door was slightly ajar. They were so busy laughing and talking they did not notice me.

I stood at the door motionless for what seemed like hours. My head felt like I was carrying the weight of the world on my shoulders. I could not gather my thoughts and my knees kept buckling beneath me.

I could not believe my eyes or ears. I tried to convince myself that it was all a dream, but I was standing there looking at them hold and caress one another. He seemed to be a very different person. They were giggling and laughing, carrying on like two school kids. The same way we were before he started taking out all of his frustrations on my body.

I couldn't figure out what to do. One minute my mind told me to run and never look back, then it was telling me to barge in there like a mad woman and attack them both. I went back and forth until I became so sick I almost vomited. Every move of my tongue I could taste bile building up. Before I knew it I was on top of his naked body attacking him in the same way he did me time after time. Now he knew what it felt like to be pounced on while you are unaware and not prepared.

Looking up at me I sensed sorrow in his eyes, he knew he had it coming. I kept wondering why he did not try to defend himself; he laid there taking every blow. It was as if he was allowing me to pay him back for everything he had done to me up until that point. At the same time he was so shocked by my actions he couldn't put together a lie. There was no way he was going to talk his way out of this. I could see the pity and shame in his eyes.

Seeing specks of blood spill from his milk chocolate skin made me feel sorry for him in that moment. I actually felt remorseful about what I was doing to him. I almost wanted to nurse his wounds and hold him in my arms.I was hurt by what he had done but I still loved him. I was no stranger to being cheated on or misused. In some ways, I had come to expect it from every man I ever entered into a relationship, which is why I preferred to be alone. My daddy and Calhoun were the only men that ever treated me like a human being. I knew they loved me.

He finally had enough and wrestled me to the ground demanding me to "calm the fuck down so I can explain this situation to you." I could not believe what I was hearing. He proceeded to accuse me of being insensitive to his needs. He even accused me caring more about Calhoun than I did him, saying, "You waited on that old man like he was God but you wouldn't keep your man satisfied. I have needs, Debbie." He yelled at me.

He was a borderline sex addict. Sex was not always an enjoyable experience for me. I told him about the sexual abuse I endured as a child but he did not seem to care. He wanted me on my back and then on my knees almost every single night except when I had my menstrual cycle. I looked forward to those five days of freedom every month. I never refused him and did as I was told even with a black eye or busted lip on occasion. Some nights were longer than others depending on how much he had to drink and smoke. If he could not perform, somehow I would be at fault.

To hear him say his needs weren't being met enraged me even more. I responded the only way I knew how which was to call him every bad name I could think of. I threw at him some of the same harsh verbal insults he had always hurled at me. I decided to let go of every pain and every hurt he had ever put me through. This was my moment to unleash on him. I felt safe in doing so because I did not think he would be cold hearted enough to beat on me in front of her. The sympathy I had for him was now gone.

She stood in the corner watching our altercation screaming, hollering and shaking like a leaf. She was so upset she couldn't put her clothes on. I kept threatening her saying, "You're next, bitch, so get ready." I was going to make her feel the same pain that I was feeling. She knew he was living with me but that did not stop her from being dirty enough to keep a sexual relationship going with him. And she welcomed him to move in with her knowing he was in a relationship with me.

Out of breath he released me from his firm grip. I did not waste any time making my way over to her. She was no match for me. Although I was small in stature I knew how to fight. I had fought men bigger than her before. She would not fight me back. Instead she went down to the ground in the fetal position holding her hands over her face.

He was too weak to pry me off her. I could hear his breathing was labored so I did not rush my attack on her. I told her all about his abusive ways, his drug habit, and how he had been living off me and Mr. Calhoun. She could not respond, she just laid there and cried like a baby. In some way I hoped my revelations would lead her to put him out or ask him to leave. I also wanted to send him the message that he needed me. I provided his livelihood.

I was jealous because he seemed to be more concerned about her than he was with me. She was short and chunky with medium length hair. She seemed like a business woman - the type who wouldn't look twice at him, not because he was on drugs but because he could not provide for her. I wondered what she wanted with Kevin. He did not have much to offer her.

Finally, he mustered up enough strength to pull me off her. She got her clothes on enough to run out of the bedroom door with her breasts exposed. I took some satisfaction in her being scared to stand up to me. I got a few more licks in on her before she darted out of the door. She did not attempt to come back at me. He shielded her from me; I was pulling at her while he was pushing her out the door with all of his might. I kept yelling at her, "Don't let me see you in the streets, bitch."

He yelled to her, "Call the police, Pam. Go call the police now!" He demanded keeping one eye on me and one eye on the door. He made sure to maintain a barrier between the door and me. He had me cornered so that I could not attack her any further.

He did not want her to get hurt. He even absorbed many of my wild misguided punches aimed at her. This let me know that he cared for her a great deal. She was not a fly by night fling that would fade away. He cared about this woman and planned to be with her. He may have even been in love with her. He was not begging for my forgiveness or asking me to come home. Instead, he was upset that I was upsetting their romantic evening.

Once she was out of the bedroom, I asked him, "So it's like that Kevin? Are you really going to send me to jail after all we have been through? Rather after all you have put me through?" Tears began to stream down my eyes as I recalled all of the beatings and all the times I forgave him.

Now I stood in the bedroom of another woman he left me for and the police were nearby.

Even then he did not beg my forgiveness or show any emotion toward me at all. He mumbled, "I think it's about that time I move on and you need to do the same." He then motioned for me to leave the apartment before the police arrived.

As I headed toward the back door he flatly said to me, "Take care, Debra." Heartbroken, I disappeared into the darkness shedding tears along the way as I tried to process what just happened. I also needed to contemplate my next move because rent would be due soon. I did not even ask about the money that he took because I knew there was no chance of me getting it back and I could not prove he was responsible for taking it.

Snow began to fall as I walked passed West Pullman Elementary School, then Kurt's store on the corner of 119th Street and Union, on my way to Butler's lounge which was almost home for me. Chicago could be so beautiful at night when fresh snow was falling from the sky. I noticed my

footprints were the first set of footprints to disrupt the snow

covering the ground.

Chapter 13

I did not sleep a wink that night. I was so sick with heartache I even vomited a few times. My mind could not break away from imagining what they were doing. Images of them smiling and loving one another kept popping up in my head. I laid there in the bed we once shared, smelling a mixture of his cologne and my perfume as I looked up to the sky questioning my faith and asking God why me. I wondered when I would get my day in the sun. My whole life had been one tragedy after another. I had a lifetime of pain but only rare moments of sunshine. Until then I took all of the bad in stride believing a blessing would be coming - now I was not so sure.

Days and weeks passed without a word from him. He seemed to have dropped off the face of the earth. Little by little I put my life back together. At night I cried myself to sleep as my mind tortured me into thinking about him and his interactions with her. He left behind a t-shirt that still had his scent on it, I would lay this on my pillow case and imagine he was there with me.

Dealing with the loss of Kevin somehow made me want to use drugs less. I was still using drugs but not nearly as much as I had when he was around. Nothing was enjoyable to me anymore because he was not there. I stayed home a lot more and did not interact as much with anyone associated with my old life. I even started reading the Bible in an attempt to draw closer to God.

I was slowly starting to heal emotionally when he showed up unexpectedly after he had been gone for about three months. There he was stretched out sleeping on the hallway floor with all of his belongings. He looked pitiful. The sun shined bright off his baldhead. He looked so sweet and innocent laying there on the dirty floor with his face partially covered by his leather jacket.

I had made up in my mind that I was over the hurt and pain he caused me, but seeing him in person made all those feelings of longing and missing him reappear. I thought I buried those feelings, but they came back like they never truly left me. I convinced myself not to overact and give in to him too easily. He still had to pay for what he put me through. I stepped over his body as if he were not there making sure to lightly tap him with my foot as I continued on out the door with my errands.

By the time I returned he was awake and sitting up. He was deep in thought and it appeared he was rehearsing what he planned to say to me. The moment he laid eyes on me the tears started flowing. "Listen, Debbie, I know I fucked up." He said grabbing my arms before I could take a swing at him. He knew I had a tendency to get violent with him, especially during moments like this where I knew I had the upper hand and could get away with throwing a few hits at him.

"Look, I know you're angry with me and you have every right to be." He blurted out as if he were reciting a speech he took weeks to prepare.

"I am a changed man and in my transition I know that my heart lies with you. She did not mean anything to me and that is why I am here now." He said looking me square in the eyes. The tears streamed steadily from his eyes. "Please, baby, give me another chance. I thought about you every single day that I was away." He sobbed to me as he tried to cup my head into his hands while trying to kiss me on the lips.

He did not know it but I was having a hard time convincing myself to not let up and punish him. My head was telling me to continue into the apartment and forget about him but my heart missed him terribly.

I would not allow myself to respond to anything he said. I remained stoic and half-heartedly tried to break away from him so that I could enter the apartment. He fought to block my path as he begged my forgiveness, even getting on his knees at one point. For a little while I listened to my head. But unfortunately, I had already decided that I would take him back but I could not do it right away.

I toughed it out and made him sleep there on the hallway floor for another week. Truthfully, I suffered more than he did. Each night I worked to convince myself not to make it easy by allowing him back in too soon. I wanted to send the message that my feelings weren't to be toyed with. I also wanted him to know I wasn't willing to deal with that kind of hurt he put me through ever again. At the same time I was testing my own strength and trying to discover if I could go on with life without him.

When I decided enough was enough I flung open the front door to the apartment and motioned for him to come in. He was still there in the hallway as if he knew I would eventually give in. His eyes perked up like a kid on Christmas as he realized the wait was over. Before I allowed him to move his belongings back in I sat him down for a lecture, much like a father would do a son who's heading out into the world for the first time.

He listened intently as I poured my heart out explaining how deeply I loved him. I tried my best to explain to him about the pain I endured throughout the course of our relationship to that point. I explained how I was fed up with being abused, used, and mistreated and made demands on how I wanted him to change. I also threatened this was absolutely the last time I would be forgiving. I promised to move forward with my life and never look back at the next sign of trouble, no matter how big or small.

Thinking back on it I was trying to convince myself that I reached my limit just as much as I was trying to sway him to love me the same way I loved him. I figured if I tugged at his heartstrings enough he'd understand the depth of my anguish. I was hoping he had sewn his wild oats and could move past his womanizing ways. For Pete's sake, the man was approaching 50 years old!

All was good for a long while between the two of us. He had even proposed marriage one Saturday afternoon while we were sitting around the apartment enjoying each other's company. We planned to go down to the courthouse and get it done for cheap. I fantasized at the mere idea of being his wife and daydreamed about the good times that seemed to lie ahead. I was the happiest I had ever been in my entire life. This was by far the longest amount of time we'd been this happy without any hiccups or drama.

Then out of nowhere, I began to get a nagging and uneasy feeling alerting me something was not right. I could not shake that feeling even as I desperately tried to persuade myself it was all in my own head. Things had been going so well I lead myself to believe something must have been wrong. Deep down I knew something was wrong, but I couldn't quite figure out what it was.

I decided to sit back and observe his every move. I soon came to realize I had been living with rose colored shades on which had me overlooking all of the dirt he was doing right under my nose. I was so happy to have him back home that I did not realize he was sneaking out at night again for hours at a time while I was sleeping. He was also creeping off to the bathroom to take his phone calls.

Slowly he began to complain about feeling stressed and being filled with anxiety. He was snippy and seemed to be searching for excuses to go out alone claiming he needed fresh air. All of this did not surprise me because I was more than accustomed to his Dr. Jekyll and Mr. Hyde personality.

He was two people occupying one body at the same time. Over the years I learned how to manage and cater to each of them.

Careful not to let him know I was aware of his changing faces I continued to act normally. I answered to his every disposal but remained focused on unveiling his secret. I wanted to catch him dead in his tracks so he could not deny anything. He always conveniently found ways of blaming me for his misdeeds. Based on what I knew about him I concluded he either met another woman or he was back to messing around with Pam. He had a gift for charming the clothes off unassuming women.

Over the next several weeks my answer finally came. The month was November and by then we were living in his daughter's, Deanna, basement. We moved in to help her care for her three small children while she worked. I quickly became fully immersed in the lives of his kids and grandkids so much that they all referred to me as mom and grandma.

I had always had somewhat of a bond with them and even the kid's mother, Brenda. I grew closer to each of them

144

because we saw them all on a daily basis. Deanna's house is where everyone gathered to hang out, especially during the summers. We frequently held cookouts and played cards on the patio in the backyard. We always had a good time and even attracted the company of neighbors. People enjoyed our company and clamored to hang out with us. We always had a large crowd of people whenever we held a gathering.

On the Friday evening before Thanksgiving, we had a family gathering for his grandson's, Daniel, 16th birthday. Kevin and I spent hours decorating the townhome and preparing his favorite dishes. The smell of fresh fried chicken and catfish filled the air.

This party started the same as all the other parties did. We had the music playing on full blast, a good card game of spade going, and the Chicago Bulls basketball game on the big screen with the volume on mute while the kids ventured throughout the three story townhome. The older kids huddled up in the corner laughing amongst each other while the younger ones ran throughout.

Between the laughter of the kids and the rowdiness of the card games, I could barely hear myself think. Since I always played the host, I was back and forth at the front door letting people in and fixing plates of food. I noticed he seemed to be on edge and would not sit still. Every few minutes he was up on his feet looking out the small kitchen window. If I didn't know any better I would have assumed he was coming down off a high. This did not make sense because we both had been clean since moving in with Deanna.

He also could not seem to part ways with the telephone, which was ringing every two - three minutes. Fed up with the suspense I stayed close to him and followed close behind wherever he went. When he disappeared into the bathroom with the telephone in hand I stood by the door and listened as best I could.

"Please don't come over here, Pam. I just need a few more days." He yelled into the phone. "Don't pull this shit on my grandson's birthday!" He pleaded. Even over the loud music and background noise, I heard him loud and clear.

My heart started to beat quickly, I thought I going to pass out. Before I could gather myself, I burst through the door and charged at him. I flung my fists as hard and fast as I could in the direction of his face. He looked at me shocked as I landed punch after punch to the right side of his face. He just stood there for a brief moment in a daze as if his feet were stuck in mud.

I could hear her shouting his name threw the phone, "Kevin! Kevin! Kevin! What is going on?" This only fueled my anger. We began to tussle, knocking down the shower curtains and all of the decorations on the walls. The commotion drew the attention of the others and before long the small kids were standing at the door screaming and crying while the adults worked to pull us apart.

A shouting match ensued and I proceeded to air all of his dirty laundry revealing every secret I knew about him. When I blurted out about the time I caught him dressing in drag everyone stopped and the room came to an eerie silence. Nobody even bothered to stop the damaged CD that skipped repeatedly on the same song in the background. This reaction is what let me know I had taken it too far. After a long unnerving moment, he shot me a hot look of contempt and calmly walked down the basement stairs to our bedroom.

A few minutes later he emerged with a wooden bat in his hand. Then he slowly walked in my direction, laid the bat down, and proceeded to savagely beat me. He was in such a rage that there was nothing I, or anyone else, could do to stop him. With all of the men out on a beer run I was at the mercy of the women and young boys. They were not strong enough to pry him off me. He yelled obscenities and berated me for talking so much.

His talking only seemed to fuel his rage. Eventually he seemed to grow tired causing the others to relent in their pursuit to stop him. Realizing this he quickly grabbed the bat and swung it with such force I could hear a swirl of wind before it connected with my skull. *Bang!* He hit me over the top of my head and everything went dark. I was sure my life was over.

Chapter 14

As I laid there in and out of consciousness, I could hear the panic of our grandkids as they screamed in horror thinking I was dead. I could hear his children chastising him questioning, "Daddy, why did you do that to her? Why did you do that?" They cried out in unison. I heard Deanna yell at him, "Get out of here before you go to jail for life. Daddy, I think you killed her." The birthday boy, Daniel, kneeled down beside me and held my hand whispering to me, "You're going to be ok. Hold on."

The paramedics were not called in an effort to protect him, which was of no surprise to me. Moreover, because I was still breathing they concluded I would survive. From what I was told, he left with Pam that night after destroying most of my belongings.

The next day I was so hurt by the incident and Kevin's family. They just left me laying there on the floor and didn't bother to check up on me. I was especially hurt by Deanna because I thought that she would have at least moved me to the bed and cleaned me up a bit. However, I had no other choice but to ask Deanna to take me to the hospital. The severe throbbing in my head gave me cause for alarm as I remembered him hitting me with the bat. On the drive to the hospital she looked me directly in the eyes and advised me to leave her daddy and never look back, explaining how her dad would never change. She said to me, "He loves his kids and grandkids but he has a dark side that even he can't control."

I was diagnosed with a concussion and given four staples in the top of my head. The doctor explained how lucky I was to be alive because that one blow came within three inches of ending my life. In that moment I realized this man could not love me and neither did his family because they showed more interest in protecting him from the police than they did in saving my life. There was no attempt to get me medical attention.

The hospital kept me overnight for observations. I laid there alone with my thoughts and ample time to think my life through. I concluded this was my ultimate *rock bottom* and I could only go up from here if I chose to walk away from him and his family. Upon my discharge from the hospital I walked five miles to the nearest women's shelter where I had to sleep on the floor for several nights until a bed became available. From the women's shelter, I became involved with an outpatient rehab center. I never went back to Deanna's to retrieve my belongings. Instead, I took her advice and tried to forget that Kevin ever existed.

Over the course of the next year I struggled to maintain my sobriety as I adjusted to my new life. I was alone and relied on the comfort of strangers to help me through it. Nights were the worst, not only because my body craved the drugs, but also because my heart wanted him. Despite the beatings, verbal abuse, and cheating I still loved him and deep down I knew he loved me too – at least that's what I believed. I tried to reconcile in my mind that he didn't mean to harm me and he just lost control that night.

I fully expected him to track me down and beg my forgiveness like the men do in the movies, but he never showed up. From time to time I wondered about what happened to him. Although I refused to press charges against him the ER doctor warned me he would pursue the matter with the State, which would involve an investigation and could lead to Kevin doing jail time.

A few times I had to stop myself from leaving the shelter and returning to Deanna's townhome to warn him. Every time the urge came on the doctor's words came to mind, "Three more inches to the right and you'd be dead." That thought always brought back my focus. So much so, I would look at myself in the mirror each night before bed and repeat it to myself as I laid my hands over the permanent small knot left by the staples. This also gave me the strength to push through the drug cravings and my weakness for him.

One of the women I had grown close to in the shelter, who had a very similar story as my own, invited me to church. I reluctantly agreed because my belief in God was fading. Although, for a short period when Calhoun was alive my faith had grown a little, I had begun to secretly question whether God existed. Through consistently reflecting on my life being filled with so much strife and pain I told myself, from time to time, that God didn't exist. I did not believe a true God would allow my mom to choose the street life over her children or my father to die so young, not to mention all of the abuse I endured throughout my life. However, I eventually overcame my doubt through prayer and worship.

I became very active in the church during the day and I spent my nights studying to obtain my GED. School was never fun for me because I had a lot of trouble reading and writing, which left me at the mercy of others. My ex-husband and Kevin both took advantage of my low IQ. Although we were all street smart, they both had book smarts which gave each of them an upper hand over me. I was dependent on them to read and explain my mail to me and to complete paperwork.

Obtaining my GED made me feel empowered and gave me a tremendous confidence boost because I was able to handle my own business affairs. This helped in other ways as well. I finally mustered up the nerve to reconnect with my kids. I promised myself that I would not attempt to re-enter their lives until I got myself together. I was still living at the women's shelter when I worked up the courage to knock on Joanne's door to ask about my kids.

I was extremely nervous and my heart was beating so fast I could barely catch my breath. My knees shook badly, I could barely hold my balance as I stood there on the doorstep and raised my arm to ring the doorbell. I rehearsed my speech repeatedly but nothing came out when Charles Jr. opened the door and stood there in awkward silence for several moments. His big beautiful smile quickly turned into a scowl when he saw that it was me. He looked like a younger, more attractive version of his father. His pearl shaped eyes slowly glanced me over. It was as if he was trying to decide if he wanted to slam the door on me like we used to do Jehovah's Witnesses when I was growing up or if he should curse me out for obvious reasons.

Joanne eventually appeared and invited me in. She always treated me with kindness and respect, even when I did not necessarily deserve it. I learned my boys moved back to Chicago from being with their father a few years earlier, and were all scattered about the city each with families of their own. They were all doing well and leading respectable lives. I worked diligently to assimilate myself back into their lives to establish a relationship. Gradually they each accepted me but no matter what I did they all viewed Joanne as their mother.

This hurt me immensely but I had no one to blame but myself because of the choices I made. I was not there for them when they needed me the most. I took solace in being accepted and that I was able to start fresh with my grandkids, which were all very young and unaware of my past troubles. I eventually reconnected with my siblings who were all still in contact with Joanne as well. Somehow, Joanne was the glue who kept everyone together even though she was not a blood relative.

When life became too difficult at the women's shelter I was invited to live with my brother, Robert, and his family. Soon after I settled in we received news that our mother was hospitalized from a bowel obstruction. We were told her prognosis was grim.

Growing up I always thought I would rejoice in her demise. I wanted her to feel the same pain and suffering she subjected us to because she was not willing to be a mother to us. However, I struggled to fight feelings of sadness and sympathy as we made our way to the county hospital. We both remained silent, overcome with nervousness about how we would react to seeing her because we had not laid eyes on her in many years.

I almost broke down in tears upon seeing her emaciated body lying in the hospital bed. Her physical condition was evidence of her years of toiling in the streets. She had dark circles and bags underneath her round, bubble shaped eyes, her dark skin was peeling, her mouth was twisted up from years of drug abuse, and many of her teeth were missing. Her once long and curly hair was fully gray and matted to her head. She looked like a skeleton.

She sobbed lightly as we approached her bed. The sobs soon turned into a steady stream of tears as she weakly uttered our names. I, too, overcome with emotion allowed the tears to flow. Lost for words, I took her hand into mine and gave her a warm hug making sure to hold her tightly because I could sense her end was near.

I felt a strange sense of comfort in her touch as I realized all these years I convinced myself to hate her because all I wanted was to be loved by her. She whispered in a weak, soft voice, "I love you." I longed to hear those words from her my whole life. I had known my daddy loved me but it couldn't compare to having my mother's love.

In just a moment's time, those three words lifted 50 years of pain, turmoil, and grief from my psyche. I spent the next five days at her bedside comforting her and confronting my haunted past while making peace with my feelings for her. In the midst of my sadness for my mother I found a sense of inner peace and happiness. I felt as if an enormous weight was lifted off my shoulders.

I held her in my arms as she took her last breath. I decided then to allow all of my burdens to die right along with her. My mother's death allowed me the strength to look to my future with renewed focus and motivation. I have been clean for nearly two years now, not only from drugs and abuse, but also from the horrors I allowed to enter my life. I hit *Rock Bottom* and conquered my biggest demons.

ROCK BOTTOM

ABOUT THE AUTHOR

My name is Latasha Boyd, and I work as a Disability Examiner for the Social Security Administration. I have worked for the Social Security Administration (SSA) in multiple capacities since September 2007. I enjoy serving the American public.

I am a native of Chicago, IL but I grew up in Minneapolis, MN where I graduated from Edison High School in 2003. I returned to Chicago, IL to attend DePaul University where I received a BA in Communications in June 2007. I also studied Psychology. I live in Park Forest, IL with my husband and two children.

I thank everyone who took the time to read my book! Rock Bottom is my very first novel, and your support means the world to me. I would love to hear from you. Feel free to connect with me!

Connect with Latasha Boyd:
Latashaboyd44@yahoo.com
Facebook: www.facebook.com/latasha.boyd.56
Twitter: @rockbottom_lb

ROCK BOTTOM

www.ingramcontent.com/pod-product-compliance
Lightning Source LLC
Chambersburg PA
CBHW040743250626
47164CB00006BA/158